Death in
Halfmoon Bay

Death in Halfmoon Bay

LARGE PRINT

A SUZANNE RICKSON MYSTERY

By Erik D'Souza

Timbercrest Publishing

Published by Timbercrest Publishing
Cover design by Rola Sahib
Copy edited by Joyce Gram
Copyright 2019 Erik D'Souza
ISBN: 978-1-9992824-31

First Edition

Large print

Dedicated to my mother,

Madeleine D'Souza

Thank you for everything

Chapter

1

Sunday, November 29th, late

Suzanne's troubled thoughts were interrupted by a siren. It was still in the distance, yet very distinct. It was an ambulance, she was sure of it.

Suzanne put down her needlepoint and noted the time, 11:24 PM. She closed her eyes and took a deep breath. She focused on every sound, blocking out her husband's snoring from upstairs, and tracking the ambulance as it turned off the highway and along Mercer Road. She hoped it would pass by her retirement community and continue towards the marina, but no such luck. The ambulance turned onto her street and roared past her townhome. It travelled deeper into the heart of the complex. After a few moments, everything became eerily silent. She strained her ears to hear more but couldn't.

Her imagination was awash with only dire possibilities; someone she knew was either dead or dying.

Suzanne rose from her favourite, worn-in armchair, and tightened her mauve dressing gown around her waist. She climbed her stairs to the best vantage point in the home, a large bay window that peered into the hamlet. Nero, their nine-year-old French bulldog, met her there and remained quiet and obedient. He looked as if he was fighting his instincts to bark at the outside racket, but his training had taught him otherwise. He resorted to a short snort. The ambulance had turned a corner into the newer section of the community; its lights danced off the windows of the townhomes.

Maybe Regina has had a stroke. It was a sinful wish, but Suzanne couldn't help it. At least now she'd have something to confess to Father O'Brian next Sunday. But alas, it was unlikely, if only the good die young then Regina Snow was destined to live to be a hundred.

There was no point in staying inside and worrying. She traipsed into the bathroom and put in her teeth. Her younger self would have wanted to apply a little make-up and brush out her hair, but she was far past such vanities. The only question in her mind was whether to wake her husband, Charles. If she left without telling him, and he woke up inexplicably alone, he'd probably have a heart attack. And then they'd need another ambulance.

Nero followed her as she returned to the window, and he remained by her feet as she pondered the situation. Why not blame the dog? "Nero, speak."

She didn't have to ask twice. Without hesitation, Nero complied. "Warf, warf."

Just as expected, she heard Charles say, "What… what is it, boy?" A few moments later he asked, "Honey, where are you?"

"An ambulance just pulled in and went around the corner." Suzanne walked into the bedroom and gripped Charles' shoulder.

"It's probably nothing. Come to bed."

"Ambulances don't come for nothing."

Charles turned onto his side. "We can look into it in the morning. So you better get some rest now."

"Only you could sleep under such circumstances!"

"It's 11:30 at night, Suzanne. It's perfectly natural to be asleep under these circumstances."

Charles's logic had always annoyed her. His brain was wired differently from hers, and she accepted that. He needed his sleep and barring an absolute emergency, Charles would not be getting out of bed. "Nero and I are going for a stroll."

"Suit yourself." Charles rolled onto his stomach and was asleep almost instantly.

Without another word, she went downstairs, put on her warmest jacket, grabbed her cane, and along with Nero, went out to investigate.

The air was cold and damp. It'll rain again tomorrow, maybe even snow, Suzanne thought. Nero splashed through the puddles; he was visibly excited to be out for such a late-night walk.

As they approached the corner of the street, she heard a commotion. Many of the residents were outside, imparting worried glances between themselves. The ambulance was parked in front of Adeline's home. Her door was wide open. Adeline won't like that, she hates wasting energy, Suzanne thought. She spotted her closest friends, Connie and Ivan, huddled together near the front of the onlookers. Suzanne squeezed her way through and asked them, "What's happening?"

"We don't know," Ivan said.

Connie's eyes were full of tears and dread. She held a tissue close to her face.

Two paramedics emerged from the doorway. Lan, Adeline's best friend, stood behind them. They were hauling Adeline in a gurney into the back of their vehicle. An oxygen mask was strapped around her mouth. Small blessings, Suzanne thought, at least she's still alive.

Chapter

2

*Saturday, November 28th, the day before
Adeline was poisoned*

The Mahjong tile in Suzanne's hand felt warm.
She rubbed her fingers along its textured back
and contemplated her next move. She was
holding the white dragon. Adeline had once told
her that this tile symbolized freedom from
corruption. If only that were true.

She eyed her friends, smiled, and discarded
the tile.

"You know that it's bad luck to win the first
game, right?" Lan giggled. She was superstitious.
She had once told Suzanne that she always wore
red underwear to their matches because red was
the colour of luck. As if a colour can affect one's
fortune.

"You mustn't allow your rivals to know when
you have the upper hand, Suzanne," Adeline said.

Her hair was freshly permed, and she smelled of expensive perfume.

"I'm working on it," Suzanne answered. Her hair was a complete contrast to Adeline's. Suzanne had earned every grey strand, and she had no desire to conceal it. She kept her hair long and brushed it every night.

"Remind me again. Why do we play this game when she always wins?" Connie played her tile.

Adeline cringed as she picked up a tile from the wall. She looked at the piece and exhaled. Suzanne knew she was a highly competitive person and didn't like being considered second-best at anything. Although in the case of Mahjong, it was true. Suzanne had been keeping score over the past three years, and she had recently pulled ahead of Adeline. The other two ladies weren't even in the picture.

Eventually, Adeline discarded a four-circles tile and said, "Mahjong gives us a chance to catch up on our families and mutual friends."

"A polite way of saying we gossip." Suzanne grinned.

"Old ladies gossip. It's what we do. But I don't see why we need to play this ludicrous game just so that we can speak ill of our neighbours," Connie said, laughing.

"You can call yourselves old ladies if you wish, but please don't call me that," Lan said. She often liked to point out that she was the youngest of the foursome.

"Lanny, dear," Connie said. "You may be fifteen years my junior, but we order from the same seniors' menu at Ricky's. So, deny it all you like, but you're old."

"Whatever." Lan looked away and waved her hands with disdain.

The quality that Suzanne liked most about Lan was her vigour. Although Lan rarely spoke of it, Suzanne knew that she had suffered from a great deal of trauma during her early adulthood. Lan was clearly attempting to recapture the youth that she had been deprived of. The new purple streak in her hair showcased her attitude towards life.

Suzanne won the first game. Inevitably. She sat back in triumph. The other three ladies began to re-shuffle the faux-ivory tiles when Connie asked, "So Adeline, how's it going on the campaign trail? Are you still confident you'll beat Regina?"

"I know I can beat her."

"Don't count your chickens before they're hatched," Suzanne warned. She'd once been the Secret Cove strata president, just as she'd been the president of the homeowners association back in Montreal. She liked being on the team that governed her residence. She had held the reins tight and had done everything by the book.

The contingency fund had always grown, and no one complained about the monthly fees.

Then, three years ago, along came Regina Snow. Regina had run a malicious crusade to oust Suzanne, lying, spreading rumours, and undermining Suzanne at every opportunity. Despite Suzanne's best efforts at a clean campaign, she had lost by a tiny margin. But the real loss was to her reputation. It was in tatters. One rumour had stung worse than all the others combined. Although she had adamantly denied it, many of the people she had once considered friends, no longer spoke to her.

The last election had changed her. She had vowed never to enter politics again, but she could hardly sit idly by as Regina ruined the place she called home. After three years of suffering under Regina's tyranny, she convinced Adeline to run for president. At first, Adeline was hesitant, but Suzanne promised to protect her. Regina was capable of anything, and this time, she would be ready.

"I think you'll win for sure, Jei Jei," Lan said as she rubbed the dark-green, jade pendant she always wore for good luck. "Everyone likes you."

"Thank you, Mei Mei," Adeline said. "I've talked to every resident here, and most have pledged their support." Adeline and Lan were very close. They called each other Mei Mei and

Jei Jei, which translated from Mandarin into little and big sister.

"The people in the older buildings trust you more," Lan said. "Everyone knows that Regina hoards all our strata fees and pours them into the newer residences."

"People's trust doesn't always translate into their votes," Suzanne said. It was her turn to play, and she was taking her time. The conversation was distracting her.

"Stop being a sour puss." Adeline puckered her lips. "Play your tile and let's get on with it. We all know Regina is done for. You need to relax."

Suzanne hid her dismay and ignored her friend's comment. Adeline often antagonized her while they played, it was a tactic to throw her off her game. Suzanne wouldn't let herself be so easily baited. She silently put down a seven of bamboo.

"I bet she started the rumour that Adeline was skimming from the strata funds," Connie said.

Adeline had been the strata treasurer for as long as Suzanne could remember. She'd been an accountant and was meticulous about keeping the books up-to-date. The thought of Adeline falsifying records and stealing from her neighbours was preposterous.

"It doesn't matter if she did," Adeline responded. "I had an independent accountant review our books, and the rumour was quickly dismissed."

Lan discarded her tile and remarked, "If that was Regina's only strategy to discredit you, it was an epic fail. The Ice Queen shall be overthrown."

Suzanne sensed that everyone was too smug and confident in Adeline's victory. The rumour of crooked books was only a warning shot. She knew that Regina had plenty in her arsenal and wouldn't hesitate to play dirty. "Even if Regina isn't up to her old tricks, she's not likely to concede easily. I tell you the Ice Queen is up to something."

Suzanne had been the first to remark that when Regina married her second husband, Byron Snow, her name translated to "Ice Queen." The moniker had stuck among many of the residents.

"I don't know," Connie said. "The election is two weeks away, and she doesn't really seem to be trying."

"I've seen Byron out a lot. He's been campaigning for her," Adeline said.

"He must really hate that," Suzanne added as she sipped some tea. "He's not the type to be going door to door,"

"The things we do for love." Lan held her hands close to her heart. "Besides, can you imagine how miserable his life would be if she lost?"

"Not *if* she loses," Adeline said. "*When* Regina loses. Poor Lord Byron, his manor shall be a living hell."

When Regina had been dubbed the Ice Queen, Byron, her quiet and reserved husband, had not become the Ice King. Instead, he became Lord Byron, after the nineteenth-century romantic poet. He was of average height and weight, wore glasses and had no real distinguishing features. He could have made the ideal spy, his non-descript appearance blended well into any crowd.

By the end of the afternoon, everyone had had their fill of Mahjong. Adeline had dealt and won the last match, scoring just enough to be the day's victor. "It's an excellent omen," she said as her guests were preparing to leave.

"Indeed," Suzanne said. It was all she could muster. She hated losing but took solace in the fact that she was still winning the overall tally.

"That was very well played," Lan said. "Did you all notice how quiet the last game was? I could feel the tension."

"Yes, that was close," Connie said. "I almost had you, Adeline. If I had won that last game, I'd have been tied with you and Suzanne. We each would have won two games. You got lucky."

"Just like in politics, there's no room for luck in Mahjong," Adeline responded.

Suzanne bit her tongue, not wanting to offend anyone. She carefully put on her coat and felt a twinge in her hip. Spotting her tote bag in the corner, she exclaimed, "Oh, I almost forgot, I brought over your jams."

"You made your jam again?" Lan said.

Suzanne wasn't sure if Lan was excited or being sarcastic. "I've been making jam for my dearest friends every year since I moved to B.C." She flung her long, white hair from under her collar. "You'll be the first to try this batch."

"You're too kind," Lan said.

"You carried all three jars here yourself?" Connie asked. "That's too much at your age."

"I'm sixty-eight," Suzanne countered. "You're the one that needs to watch her age, not me."

"I'm a very healthy eighty-one. My doctor says I'll probably outlive him. And it wasn't me that broke her hip last year. Where's your cane? You left it at home again, didn't you."

"I only need that thing on bad days," Suzanne responded. "And it's not a bad day today, is it, ladies."

"*Au contraire*, my friends, today is a blessed day, the best of days." Adeline lifted her hands high up with adulation.

Lan sniffed the air as she opened the front door. "It even smells like a good day. Fresh and ripe for change."

"It's cold." Connie tightened her collar around her neck.

Suzanne wasn't looking forward to the walk home. Adeline's home was the farthest unit away from her own home. It was the corner unit of the newest building in the Secret Cove Retirement Community. Adeline was one of its longest inhabitants. She used to reside in one of the older units, but the developers had given the existing residents first dibs on the new, bigger townhouses. The gesture had done little to appease them, as most were adamantly opposed to any change in their tranquil lifestyle.

Suzanne had been the most vocal and had argued that it was absurd to erect three-story homes in a retirement community. Unbeknownst to her, Adeline was silently arranging the purchase of the most expensive and largest unit. It offered the quietest location, furthest from the main road, and had a spectacular view of the marina and Salish Sea.

"Has anyone else noticed the black pick-up truck that's been parked out there for a while?" Suzanne asked as she stepped outside.

"It's a dark blue truck, and it's been there for three nights," Connie corrected her.

"It's black," Suzanne said.

Lan squinted. "Stop bickering, ladies. I'd call it gray."

"You girls may be younger than me, but your eyesight is horrible," Connie said. "I know for sure that it's a blue truck because it's Regina's son's car. He often leaves it there."

Suzanne said nothing. She was fully aware that Regina's son drove a black truck. He worked as a commercial fisherman and often spent time with his mother and step-father in between jobs. It was his truck, she was sure of it, but there was no point in arguing. Her friends would see whatever they wanted to see.

"Did you know that he used to be in a gang?" Lan said.

"Where did you hear that?" Suzanne asked. She was skeptical of such a harsh accusation.

"I didn't know he was in a gang," Connie said. "But I heard that he'd served time for breaking into people's cabins up in the Okanagan."

"I don't know anything about any of that," Adeline said. She looked cold and probably wanted everybody to leave so she could close her front door. "He's a fisherman now, and he has a family."

"As if having a family makes you a good man," Connie said.

Suzanne didn't want to start arguing in the cold. She wanted to go home. "Forget the truck.

It's not important. I think we should all agree with Adeline, it's a beautiful day. Let's not ruin it."

"I second that motion," Connie said.

"How did Lanny put it?" Adeline asked. "It's fresh and ripe for change."

"Hear, hear," Suzanne said. Everyone seemed pleased that even Suzanne agreed that Adeline's victory was no longer in doubt. But Suzanne had her reservations. She was preparing herself for Regina's next move, knowing full well that it would be decisive.

Chapter

3

Monday, November 30th, early morning

"**W**ake up, Charles."

It was now past midnight. Suzanne had walked home as fast as she could with her cane. She cursed her age and missed the days when she could have jogged several kilometres without much effort.

Charles didn't stir.

Nero took his spot at the end of the bed, exhausted from his unexpected adventure. The late-night walk, a pleasant surprise, must have taken a lot out of him. He plopped down and was asleep in seconds.

Suzanne shook her husband, and he turned his back to her.

"Oh, wake up you big oaf." She pinched his shoulder.

"What is it now?" he said, far from being alert.

"It's Adeline. An ambulance came and took her away. Nobody told us anything, but they must've taken her to the Sechelt Hospital. We have to go."

Unlike earlier, Charles did not argue. He was up in a flash, dressed, and ready to go in five minutes. He was grabbing his car keys, when Suzanne said, "We're not driving. Connie and Ivan will be here any second."

A car stopped in front of their home just as she finished her sentence.

Very little was said on the way to the hospital. They speculated a bit about what could have happened to Adeline, but they were all trying to avoid the worst-case scenarios. Highway 1 didn't have many streetlights, making it very dark and isolated at night. The lack of traffic allowed Ivan to travel just over the speed limit. Ivan slowed down right before they passed by the police station, which was at the outskirts of Sechelt's city centre.

Within minutes they were on the other side of the town. Ivan parked in the handicap spot closest to the emergency room doors of the Sechelt Hospital. The last time Suzanne was here she had slipped and broken her hip.

They rushed through the ER doors in a panic, only to find a sterile room, devoid of activity. Its only occupant was the attending clerk positioned at the triage window. Everything felt disconcertingly serene.

"Was our friend, Adeline Wong, brought here a few moments ago?" Suzanne asked.

"Let me check." The clerk surely knew the answer, but haphazardly typed a few keys on the computer for show. "Are any of you family?" she eventually asked.

"No, we are all friends," Connie responded.

"Her only sister lives in Toronto," Suzanne added, hoping that would help their cause.

"She's in the ER, and the doctors are with her now. Her friend, the one who rode in the ambulance with her, is also present."

"Oh good," Suzanne said. At least Adeline wasn't alone. "Is she going to be alright?"

"I'm sorry, but I don't know anything more than that. If you'd be so kind as to take a seat, I'll try and find out more for you."

The four of them complied. Thank God the room wasn't filled with crying children and coughing adults, Suzanne thought.

The longer they sat, the more Suzanne worried.

After thirty minutes of hearing nothing, Connie got up and asked, "For heaven's sake, what's going on back there?"

"I'm sorry, I still don't know. I've requested

more information, and I've notified Ms. Hynes that you are here."

"She knows plenty, Hon," Ivan said as his wife sat back down beside him. "But she just can't tell you."

"It's preposterous that they make us wait here like this." Connie gripped her armrest tightly.

"The privacy laws in Canada are stringent," Ivan said. "They may seem burdensome in times like this, but the rules are in place to protect our personal information."

"They're a pain the rump, is what they are," Connie rebuked.

"Don't worry, dear," Suzanne spoke up. She loved Connie and Ivan and considered them her closest friends. They lived in the townhome beside her. They had introduced themselves on the day that she and Charles had moved in, nine years ago. She had quickly learnt that Ivan had served in the Canadian Navy and then worked at the Department of Defence. Connie had been a school teacher and was an active member of Greenpeace. They were the sweetest people, but at the same time, had conflicting political standpoints. They often engaged in heated debates, even in the most inappropriate situations. Suzanne didn't want them to start now. She tried to find common ground. "Regardless of what they are telling or not telling us, whatever is wrong with Adeline, the doctors are with her."

"It's probably a stroke." Charles entered into the conversation. "Or maybe it was a heart attack. Hopefully, she didn't wait too long before calling 911."

"She could have just fallen out of bed and hurt her hip," Suzanne deduced. "It's a common accident for people our age. At least it isn't fatal."

"I suppose it's possible," Connie admitted.

Just then, Lan appeared from behind a set of double swinging doors, "Oh thank God, you're all here." She hugged her friends.

"What's going on?" Connie asked. There was no concealing her irritation.

"Is Adeline alright?" Suzanne asked.

"The doctors believe that she's been poisoned."

"What? How? Is she going to live?" Suzanne's voice cracked.

"The doctors are awaiting the tox examination, but they think it might be a cardiac glycoside. They've administered her some activated coal and they have her hooked up to an electrocardiogram and an IV bag. They're doing all they can." Lan broke into tears, and the men had to hold her up. They brought her to a chair and eased her down.

"It's going to be alright," Charles said, in a soothing tone.

"Don't you see? It's not going to be okay." Lan sobbed.

Charles turned to Suzanne and asked, "What's Cardiac Glyco-something or another?"

Suzanne wasn't an expert, but she knew her fair share about poisons. She had read every word that Agatha Christie ever penned. "Cardiac glycoside is a deadly toxin. It affects the heart, stomach and nervous system. It's sometimes used as an ingredient within cardiac medicines, but only in the most minuscule of amounts. A larger dose is highly toxic. It can be fatal if the patient isn't treated quickly. Oh God, I hope they caught it in time."

Lan sobbed even louder, and Charles did his best to stop her from going completely hysterical.

"I need a coffee. Does anyone else want one too?" Ivan asked his voice was calm.

Connie scolded at him before walking away and hounding the clerk for more information.

"I'm sorry, I know as much as you do, until the doctors tell us more," the clerk repeated over and over again.

Suzanne closed her eyes and prayed. She had promised to protect Adeline from Regina. She had anticipated that the rumours would resurface, but she never imagined that Regina would outright harm Adeline.

Lan composed herself, got up and demanded to be let back into the ER room to see Adeline.

"I'm sorry, but Ms. Wong has been taken to the ICU. A specialist is with her now. I'll inform you of any changes as soon as they happen."

"Like when you informed us that she had been taken to the ICU," Connie said.

The clerk ignored her.

"At least she's with a specialist," Suzanne said. "I'm sure she's in good hands."

"She's in God's hands now. Lord, please protect her." Lan peered towards the heavens.

Suzanne was surprised. Lan was by far the least religious person present. Adeline had been trying unsuccessfully for years to get Lan to accept God's love and to start coming to Sunday mass with them.

"Typical," Connie whispered. "The heathens always call out for God's aid whenever they really need him."

"Amen," Ivan whispered back.

Connie and Ivan were two of the most devote Christians Suzanne had ever met. They donated to several charities and sponsored half a dozen children in Africa. They always exemplified good Christian behaviour. Still, every once in a while, they liked to whisper to each other something along the lines of, "Oh now she wants God to help."

Suzanne sat and waited. She wished that she had her needlepoint. A muted television hung from the corner ceiling, and the men were distracted as the ticker displayed the results of previous night's hockey scores.

Suzanne preferred to remain on the subject. She continued her prayers.

"I'll be forever lost if Adeline doesn't make it!" Lan lamented. She squeezed her jade pendent tight, just as Connie was clinging to her crucifix.

"Don't worry dear. Adeline is very stubborn and has a lot of fight in her," Suzanne said. "Remember when Regina wanted to spend our contingency fund on a hot tub. Regina had convinced everyone in the strata that it was a good idea. Everyone except Adeline that is. And see, we still don't have a hot tub."

"She persuaded us all to start playing Mahjong," Lan said. "Even though you two didn't want to try it."

Suzanne remembered the day that Adeline had introduced the game of Mahjong to the group, although she didn't recall resisting it that much.

She and Adeline had served on the strata together and become fast friends. Suzanne introduced her to Connie, and in turn Adeline brought Lan Hynes into their fold. The four of them had quickly formed a tight bond.

Suzanne later learnt that Lan had a sad and tragic past. Adeline had been doing all that she could to lift her friend up and onto her feet again. For instance, Adeline had paid for Lan's down payment of her home and often leant her money. Her kindness wasn't only financial. Lan refused to go to church, so Adeline did her best to spread the good word and show her the true depth of Christian compassion.

Three years ago, just after Suzanne lost the election and was upset, Adeline proclaimed, "We should all play Bridge together."

"I hate Bridge," Suzanne said.

"Okay then," Adeline said, undeterred. "I know the ideal game for us to play, it's nothing like Bridge. In fact, it doesn't even use cards. The ageless game of Mahjong, you'll love it."

"You're not going to give up, are you?" Suzanne had said.

"Nope."

Suzanne appreciated that her friend was trying to cheer her up. The other two ladies had agreed instantly to try it, even Connie, who wasn't fond of games.

Adeline had been right. They were all quickly consumed by Mahjong. The foursome arranged to play every Wednesday and Saturday afternoon. Adeline volunteered her living room as long as everyone else did the cooking.

During one of their earlier matches, Connie had said, "I read that the game of Mahjong was often played for money. Do you girls want to start playing for pennies?"

"NO!" Adeline shrieked.

It was only later, when Lan was no longer present, that Adeline explained. "Lan was once addicted to gambling. I shouldn't be telling you this, but she regularly attends Gamblers Anonymous meetings. She insists that it's under control, and she has promised me that she'll never gamble again.

"Do you remember when Adeline tried to cook us all an authentic Chinese meal and burnt almost everything." Connie's voice awoke Suzanne from her memories.

"She tried to convince us that was how it was supposed to be," Suzanne said with a smile.

"What kind of Asian woman can't even cook rice?" Lan laughed.

"Yet she has just about every kitchen contraption ever made," Suzanne said.

"She even had a mango slicer. All it does is cut mangos. Who would buy something like that?" Connie's voice was getting louder.

"Now to be fair, she did use that slicer a fair bit," Lan answered. "She may not have been able to cook beans, but her food presentation was always immaculate."

"Yeah, she always knew how to lay out burnt tiger prawns, I'll give her that," Connie said.

All three ladies broke into laughter. Suzanne realized that they were already referring to Adeline in the past tense, but she kept it to herself. She didn't want to upset Lan again.

They all stopped laughing when a RCMP officer, middle-aged and tall, walked through the front entrance directly to the clerk. Suzanne strained her ears, but they were speaking too quietly. The clerk pointed out their group while avoiding eye contact with them. The officer turned and smiled. Suzanne looked down at her watch; 4:17, Sunday morning. The RCMP officer took off his hat before approaching.

His voice was solemn. "I'm sorry to inform you, but your friend, Adeline Wong, has passed away."

Lan fainted. Charles had to catch her. The officer said something about having to speak to them all in the near future, but Suzanne couldn't focus her attention. She too was feeling very light-headed and had to close her eyes. "She's in God's hands now," she whispered to herself.

Chapter

4

Wednesday, December 2nd, early afternoon

Torrential rain had drenched Suzanne's garden for the past couple of days. It finally stopped earlier that morning, but the overcast skies persisted. Suzanne sat stoically in her den, settled on her favourite armchair with the curtains drawn and the lights turned off. She was alone. Jazz played quietly in the background. She had been crying for days but now forced herself to stop. Suzanne cleared her head. She needed to mentally review everything that had happened.

Charles had remained beside her ever since the original shock. For two days, he had been a comforting rock for her to weep upon. But he needed to mourn too, and he never liked crying in front of her. He had left early in the morning for a walk and had been gone for hours. She knew not to worry, for he would eventually return a revived man, once again a pillar to lean upon.

Nero must have been somewhere in the house, but he remained silent and scarce. That was until the doorbell rang. He barked only once and ran to the front door. She ignored the commotion. It was probably Lan needing to grieve with her again, but Suzanne didn't want to talk anymore. She wanted to be left alone.

On the second ring, Nero started running in circles in the kitchen.

"Hold your horses, I'm coming," Suzanne hollered.

Suzanne had dreaded their arrival but knew it was inevitable. The police had draped yellow tape outside Adeline's home, and they were treating it as a crime scene. They had been canvassing the neighbourhood for two days, and it was only a matter of time before they rang on her door. She wished that Charles was still home.

The young man standing outside her door was tall and lean. His hairline was starting to recede even though he looked as though he was in his mid-thirties. His uniform was recently pressed. He exuded confidence and authority.

She opened the door to him, pretending not to know who he was. Even though they had never met, Suzanne had read plenty in the community newspaper, The Coast Reporter, about the new staff sergeant from Montreal who had been recruited into the Sechelt RCMP. Suzanne had only seen lesser ranked officers canvassing the complex. She wondered why he came in person to talk to her. Perhaps he'd learnt of her reputation for being shrewd and keen, and wanted her insight.

"Hello," Suzanne said warmly, recapturing her composure.

"*Bonjour*, Ms. Rickson. My name is Staff Sergeant Laval. I'm a member of the RCMP, and I'm the lead investigator in your friend Adeline Wong's death. May I come in?" His accent was distinct. It was clear that he was proud of his French heritage.

"Hello. Yes, please come in." She opened the door wide for the officer. The front of the home had no foyer and led directly into the kitchen. Suzanne beckoned him to sit at the kitchen table and offered him a cup of coffee. He declined.

"Are you sure? I was just about to make a cup for myself." It was an innocent lie. She often praised herself for having a high degree of hospitality.

The staff sergeant must have sensed this, for he asked, "If you don't mind, I much prefer tea. Green if you have it."

"Then you're in luck, Staff Sergeant," Suzanne said. "My husband and I love tea. Our daughter Lisa buys us a delightful jasmine tea from a quaint, little Asian teashop in Vancouver.

I'd love to make you some." Calm down, she thought. Remember to breathe.

"Yes, if it's no trouble. That sounds lovely."

"Great, I'll have some too."

While the tea was brewing, Staff Sergeant Laval said, "Ah, Ms. Rickson, you have good taste in music: Oscar Peterson. Did you know that he was a French Canadian, like us?"

Of course, she knew that Oscar Peterson was born in Montreal, every Canadian jazz enthusiast knows that. But what puzzled Suzanne was something else, "How did you know that I was from Quebec?"

"You still have the faintest trace of an intonation," Laval informed her.

"I was born in Montreal. My husband, Charles, worked in construction and his company moved out west after the first referendum. That was over thirty-five years ago." At the time, she had mixed feelings about moving to the West Coast. The majority of her family lived in Quebec, but she knew that she had little choice. Times were far too tough to quit a good paying job, and she was pregnant with their first child.

After settling in Vancouver, Suzanne only spoke English. No one had picked up on her French inflection for at least two decades. Suzanne liked the young detective; he was clearly a perceptive man.

"It's the way we pronounce our H's. We French Canadians pronounce them quite distinctly from our English cousins." Laval said. "But, alas, I am not here to discuss our mutual heritage. I wish I were. I have been made aware of your relationship with the deceased, Adeline Wong."

Laval must fancy himself as a young Hercule Poirot. Suzanne held back her urge to chuckle. "Yes, we were good friends," she responded.

"I was also informed that you liked to gossip amongst your companions."

Was he testing her? Trying to push her buttons? "It's true that I like to know the coming and goings of those around me. What old lady doesn't? Living in a retirement community is very much like being in high school all over again. Knowledge is a commodity."

Staff Sergeant Laval didn't hold back his laughter; he chuckled like a free spirit. Suzanne missed the *joie de vivre* that the French possess. "I assure you, young man, I collect information far more than I circulate it. Some people in this community love to stir the pot. I, on the other hand, prefer to keep to myself."

"Still, perhaps you could share with me some of that information you've collected. As in, who do you suppose would want to harm Ms. Wong?"

One name popped into Suzanne's head immediately. But it wouldn't be prudent to just blurt it out. She mustn't impose her biased opinion upon this officer. He must come upon it himself. "Sadly, ex-husbands are always a good place to start. Statistically speaking husbands or exes are often the perpetrators of violence against their wives. Have you interviewed Anthony Wong?"

"We have."

Suzanne had never met Anthony, and Adeline rarely spoke of him. Several years ago, Adeline had said, "That snake left me for a young secretary in his accounting firm. He destroyed me, and because of him, I will never trust a man again."

Suzanne was curious to know if he was a suspect. "Did he provide you with an alibi?" she asked.

The officer didn't reply. Instead, he asked, "Were you aware that a Lan Hynes is the heir to Ms. Wong estate? I find it odd that she left nothing to her biological sister in Toronto."

The Staff Sergeant was watching her keenly. Her reaction was just as what she might say. She maintained her serenity. "She was not close to her real sister. I don't think they've spoken in years. Lan and Adeline, on the other hand, were very close. They cared for each other very much."

32

"Thank you, I also got that impression," the officer said. He lifted his little finger as he sipped his tea before continuing. "Is there anything else of note that you'd like to add at this time?"

Suzanne didn't quite like the tone of this last question. Was he suspecting that she was withholding information? "There's a lot that I could tell you," she responded. "It's really just a question of figuring out what's relevant and what isn't."

"Please, ma'am, tell me everything and let me determine what's relevant."

"Well alright," Suzanne took a moment to ponder which tidbit to introduce next. "There was this black pick-up truck parked at the end of the strata for several days. During the summer months, it's not uncommon for people to illegally park in our lot and spend the day at the marina. Hikers sometimes leave their vehicles here for a week as they trek along the coast. It drives us mad. We often call the city to have their cars towed away. If you ask me, we should... I'm sorry. Look at me, I'm getting carried away."

The parking situation infuriated Suzanne. Her suite stood at the entrance of the Secret Cove Retirement Community, and she had an excellent vantage point of the visitor's parking lot. She had self-appointed herself the de facto sentry of the complex and recorded the vehicles that stayed overnight. She had noted the pick-up and jotted down its license plate number, which she had long ago memorized.

Still, she found it odd that Laval hadn't interjected. He was looking directly at her. He appeared to be making mental notes of every word she said, and every little movement she made. "What I meant to say is that people don't usually leave their vehicles here for extended periods in the winter. A few of us observed it, but we didn't call the city. It was a black Dodge. It was parked for three days and left the night before Adeline died."

"I see." Staff Sergeant Laval gestured for her to go on.

"Has anyone else told you about this vehicle? I believe it's important." Suzanne asked.

Laval nodded. "A neighbour of yours had witnessed a similar vehicle, although they had reported that it was dark blue."

Of course she had. Suzanne couldn't take it anymore. She couldn't help but ease the detective onto the path that he should be taking. "Well, you see our, strata president, Regina, her son drives a pick-up just like it. I've been told that he has a criminal record."

"That's Regina Snow, is that correct?"

"Yes it is," Suzanne answered. "Have you spoken to her yet?"

"*Oui Madame*, I have. What can you tell me about her?"

Suzanne didn't know where to start. "As I already mentioned she's the strata president. Back home we have a Homeowners Association for multifamily complexes, here we have stratas…"

"*Oui*, I know, Ms. Rickson. Carry on."

Suzanne was getting flustered. She took a deep breath. "Well anyways… I believe she's on her second marriage. She had married a wealthy older man when she was just a teenager. He passed away and left her everything…"

"Actually Ms. Rickson," Laval stopped her again. "Mr. Travis Hudson is very much alive."

"Who?"

"Mr. Hudson was her first husband. He lives in Kentucky."

"Really?" Suzanne was surprised. Her eyes rolled to the side as she tried to remember who told her that Regina was once widowed. "I'm sorry… I guess it's like I said, rumours spread like the plague at Secret Cove."

"Indeed." Laval looked up into her eyes. "I've also heard a rumour. It's been said that your husband, Charles, once had an affair with the deceased."

And there it was. The rumour that ruined her three years ago. She knew it wouldn't stay buried. At least one person had re-hashed it and brought it the attention of the RCMP. Was she now a suspect? Was that why the staff sergeant was questioning her in person? "I haven't heard that one in a while. Not since Regina spread it in order to tarnish my reputation during the strata elections three years ago. Was she the one who told you that?"

"Do you deny the rumour?" Laval asked, once again ignoring her question.

How rude, she thought, but then again it is standard police procedure for controlling an interview. She couldn't let him manipulate her, she had to maintain control. "Of course I do. Charles isn't the type of person to betray anyone, let alone me. It's absurd. But I expect no less these days."

"I have no doubt that your husband is above reproach. Would you say the same of Ms. Wong?"

It was a loaded question. A trap. She sipped her tea, "Adeline and I had been friends for six years, ever since we were on the strata council together. We talked nearly every day, and she never struck me as the type of person to ever harm a friend. But in many ways, I feel as though I never really knew her. She was very guarded."

"I see," Laval said. "One last question, if you don't mind. What can you tell me about Murray Wilthe?"

Of course Murray is a suspect, she thought. I bet lots of people think he may have done it. "Regardless of what anyone has said about him,

Murray's a nice man. He's a touch offbeat, but overall very kind. He works at the Rona hardware store in Sechelt and often helps out around here doing little chores. I believe that he had once wanted to marry Adeline, but it was before I knew her."

"Would you know his whereabouts?"

"No, I wouldn't. Charles might, but he's not in."

"Is your husband a close friend of Mr. Wilthe?" Laval asked.

Suzanne pondered her response before revealing, "I don't think Murray has any good friends. He's a quiet man. My husband, on the other hand, is friends with anyone he's ever met."

Almost on cue, the front door opened. Nero, who'd been sitting patiently, erupted with joy as Charles stumbled through the door. Suzanne quickly introduced the two men so that Charles would know who he was addressing.

"I trust you haven't been driving," Staff Sergeant Laval said as he rose from his chair.

"No, Officer, I was walking."

It's no surprise that Charles would be grieving at the pub. She hugged Charles, gauging to what degree he was inebriated. A sober Charles was always polite and kind, but put a few pints in him, and he became the centre of attention. A few more pints and he slips back into a British accent. If he tilts the scotch, he might say a few inappropriate things before passing out.

"I hope you didn't overdo it, honey," Suzanne said heartily.

"No, not at all. You know me dear, I'm a lightweight."

"So you say," she guffawed. "I'll make you some tea. Staff Sergeant, can I offer you another cup?"

"*Non merci*, Ms. Rickson. You have been all too kind. But, alas, I really should be on my way."

Suzanne smiled. She loved receiving affirmation of her generous hospitality. She also noticed that Laval had no intention of questioning Charles. He had come specifically to speak to her. Was this a preliminary interrogation concealed as a polite interview?

"You should stay just a little longer, Officer," Charles said. "Obviously you were here to speak about Adeline's death. Did you know that she had life insurance and listed Murray Wilthe as beneficiary?"

"The insurance company notified the RCMP right away," Staff Sergeant Laval said. His eyes tightened before he asked, "But I am curious as to how you discovered this, Mr. Rickson?"

"He told me himself, just now."

"Really, and where was this?" Laval's tone perked up.

"At the Dockside Pub," Charles answered. "Do you know it? It's at the far end of the marina."

"*Oui*, I know it," Laval responded. "Well, as I said, I should be off. *Adieu.*"

"He was in a hurry," Charles said after the two of them had settled down, each with a cup of fresh tea.

"Off to the Dockside no doubt," Suzanne said.

"I don't know if he'll catch Murray. He was calling a cab just as I was leaving."

"Tell me, did Murray seem surprised that Adeline left him some life insurance money?"

"Ah … yeah, he seemed genuinely shocked. Although, it was hard to say for sure. He was really drunk and kept repeating, she really did love me. He was pretty much crying most of the time. Poor guy … does it matter if he knew or not."

"Yes, dear, it does. It's the difference between having a motive or not."

"Surely, you don't think Murray killed Adeline."

"Well, somebody did."

Chapter

5

Mid-afternoon

"**S**top panicking, Mom."

"I'm not panicking, I'm fine," Suzanne retorted into the phone.

"I know you, Mom," Caroline said. "A police officer comes for an interview, so you assume the worst: that they've already pegged you as the prime subject. You have to watch your blood pressure."

"My heart is fine. I take pills, and it's not an issue. What is an issue is that he didn't mention my jam. He should have asked for it in order to test it."

"Mom, you can't believe that it was your jam that poisoned her. She could have eaten anything. In fact, the poison may not have been ingested at all."

"I'm sure it was. You see, when Lan was at the hospital, she heard a doctor say cardiac glycoside overdose. Glycosides taste sweet. The killer would've had to add it to something sugary. My jam was a perfect choice."

"Are you sure she heard the doctor say exactly that? It's pretty technical."

"You forget that Lan was a dental hygienist. She's right at home with all these medical terms. My knowledge of it comes from literature. Have you ever read *Appointment With Death*?"

"Mom, just because you read a lot of mystery books doesn't make you an expert."

"I looked it up on the internet to learn more. In fact, I have just discovered that lilies of the valley were Agatha Christie's favourite flower."

"Wait, back up, you went online?" Caroline snickered.

"Okay smarty pants, your father did. And this is what we discovered: glycosides are organic, found in many garden plants like foxglove and lily of the valley. Of course, I knew those plants were poisonous, so I never grew them in my garden."

"Of course, you knew that."

"Watch your tone, I'm still your mother." Too many years in the army and then in the police force had jaded Caroline.

"Sorry."

"I may not have known all the details of the toxin, but I know which plants are poisonous and which aren't. But plenty of other gardeners grow them. In fact, they can even grow in the wild here in the Pacific Coast."

"Okay fine, let's presume that Adeline was poisoned by a plant. You still can't assume that it was mixed in your jelly."

"My jam, dear. There's a difference. Jellies use only the juices of the fruit, and they take out all the seeds and fibre. It's all sugar..."

"Whatever Mom, stick to the point."

"Don't whatever me." Suzanne raised her voice. "You should know these things."

"Alright, I'm sorry, again," Caroline said. She sounded dejected. She had once called her mother a drill sergeant, rigid and unrelenting. She inhaled and continued, "You can't just assume that your jam was poisoned."

"I don't just assume things, dear. Someone snuck into Adeline's home and poisoned my jam between the hours of eleven AM and one PM on the day that Adeline passed away."

"Wow, now you're getting very specific."

"I've been thinking about it a lot. I'm fairly certain that it was my blackberry jam that was tainted."

"Okay fine, tell me why you are so sure."

"Because before Lan discovered Adeline in a

coma upstairs, she noticed a single dish in the kitchen sink. The dish had bread crumbs on it and some dark jam."

"But she still could have eaten something else too."

"Could have, maybe, but I doubt it. We all had lunch together after noon mass. It was a soup and salad fundraiser. We had our fill and Adeline was to meet Lan later for dinner. The jam sandwich was just a tiny snack." Suzanne shifted her weight on the sofa. Her hip was getting sore again.

"Alright fine, I get it, but not all poisons react instantly. She could have ingested it the night before and only succumbed to it the day after," Caroline said.

"Please dear, you're a police officer; you should know your poisons better."

"I'm a suspended police officer in East Vancouver. I've seen my fair share of drug overdoses and bullet wounds, but people don't go around poisoning each other. That kind of stuff only happens in the books that you read. You're not Miss Marple, you know."

"Are you done?"

"No..... Yes. Okay. Fine."

"Alright then, just listen. Adeline was a little neurotic. She preferred the term eccentric, but still, it's all the same thing. One of her many quirks was that she couldn't leave a dirty dish in the sink. Everything had to be tidy and in its place. So here's what I think happened. After coming home from mass, Adeline wanted a snack, so she went into her kitchen, made herself a jam sandwich, washed the knife and put it away. She sat down to eat and felt ill almost instantly. Glycosides act fast; she would have experienced nausea and an upset stomach. That's why she didn't clean and put the dish away. She never would've imagined that she was poisoned. Lan called her shortly after and Adeline cancelled their dinner plans because she was coming down with something. Poor Lan, she blames herself. If she had checked up on Adeline and taken her to the hospital sooner, the doctors may have been able to save her." Suzanne was pleased to have been able to state all her facts without interruption. She paused to let Caroline speak.

"It's not her fault. Lan couldn't have guessed that Adeline was poisoned."

"Of course Lan couldn't have known, but none the less she's in a terrible place, thinking of all the things that she could've done differently. Really it was Adeline's foolishness; she should've phoned 9-1-1 right away."

"Don't blame the victim. It's not her fault someone poisoned her."

"Ah, so you are coming around."

"Fine, yes, I'll agree with you. But what about the window of opportunity you gave? What was it you said, between eleven and one? How did you get that?"

"Because Adeline had eaten some of my jam for breakfast. She told me right before mass that she really enjoyed it. We go to church every Sunday, and we're gone between eleven and one PM. The killer must have known this."

"That sounds feasible," Caroline said.

"See, I told you that I don't just assume things."

"Sure you do, you assume that people are always telling you the truth. In my line of work, I've learnt that people often lie."

"I know. I was reminded of that first hand earlier today." Suzanne was still very much annoyed about telling the young staff sergeant a rumour regarding Regina that she hadn't confirmed. Lesson learned. Yet she felt confident in saying, "Adeline wasn't lying. She told me that it was much better than last years. I had added blueberries last year, and it didn't go over well. Adeline was pleased that I had gone back to my old recipe."

Caroline sighed, and Suzanne continued. "Our killer gained access to her home while we were all out, poisoned my jam and left undetected."

"Our killer?"

"Yes, our killer. I need you to find out if the police have found any signs of forcible entry."

"Mom, I'm suspended. And even if I wasn't, I couldn't divulge any official details while the investigation is still active."

"Stop playing games with me. Suspended or not, you still have plenty of friends on the force. Caroline dear, this is very important… Oh! And find out if the lab has discovered anything about the poison."

"No."

"Ask your Indian friend, what's her name? The one who wants to live with you."

"Alright that's enough, I have to go."

"Get me the information," Suzanne insisted. She needed her daughter's help.

"I'll see what I can do, but I'm not breaking any protocols for you. It could jeopardize the case, and I'm in too much trouble as it is."

"Fair enough, I love you, honey."

"I love you too, Mom – oh wait, before you go, did you and Dad decide on Christmas?"

"Yeah, I guess we'll go," Suzanne said.

"Great, Lisa will be overjoyed. I'll tell her to buy the tickets."

"I'm still not thrilled about it. Your father and I are perfectly capable of getting ourselves back to Montreal, to see your grandfather."

"Lisa wants to do it. Besides, what's the point of having lots of money if you never spend it? She and Mark are trying to be nice."

"If you say so," Suzanne said.

"Stop being a sourpuss. I'll see you later, Mom."

"Goodbye."

****

After her phone call to Caroline, Suzanne wanted nothing more than a hot bath. But she had work to do. Her mind was racing, and she needed to talk to Lan. Her discussion with Staff Sergeant Laval raised many new questions. The pleasure of a warm, relaxing soak would have to wait.

She grabbed her cane and left Nero at the door. "Sorry boy, not this time."

Opening the front door let in the fragrant smell of winter jasmine. This pleased Suzanne and boosted her spirit. She took in a large breath through her nose, held it and exhaled through her mouth. Always remember to breathe. It was the advice given to her from her doctor and had become her mantra. It helped keep her blood pressure low.

The sky was still dark, and it was starting to drizzle. Suzanne opted to wear her hood as to not frazzle her long hair. She navigated the puddles with little difficulty and arrived at Lan's home, only four doors down from hers.

No one answered the door. She should've called first. Maybe Lan doesn't want any visitors. Too bad, she needed answers. She rang the doorbell again and waited. Still nothing.

Suzanne noticed the curtain move in the adjacent townhome. It was Elizabeth Fisher, who had once been a charming woman. Mr. Fisher, on the other hand, had been a boisterous man who drank too much and smoked two packs a day. He had passed away six years ago, leaving Elizabeth all alone to fend for herself.

Since then Elizabeth spent the majority of her time by her front window, all dolled up as if she was going to the theatre. But instead of going out, she remained by the window. Suzanne figured that this was her theatre, everyday people coming and going past her home. Elizabeth rarely ever said hello to her, or to anyone else for that matter. Other than Charles of course; he was friendly with everyone in the complex. But today, without Charles as an escort, Elizabeth sat blankly, oblivious to Suzanne's presence.

"Have you seen Lan?" Suzanne hollered.

The old woman's eyes were blank, like a figure in Madame Tussaud's Wax Museum.

Oh come on. "Elizabeth, do you know where she is? Her car is here, but she's not answering the door."

Elizabeth raised her hand and pointed to Building C.

It's a good thing that Suzanne had her cane with her, for the walk from Lan's to Adeline's was quite the trek. She'd have to walk the length of both the original structures and then take a left and travel to the last townhome in the new building.

While on her way, she passed the Hendersons, who had very little to say to her other than, "We're terribly sorry about your loss." There was a time when Suzanne had considered them to be close friends, now they barely spoke.

Suzanne could feel her hip starting to hurt as she stood in Adeline's doorway. She felt awkward ringing the doorbell as if her departed friend would somehow emerge and greet. Instead, she tried the knob. To her surprise, the door opened.

"Hello, Lan?" she bellowed.

"Suzanne? Is that you?" Lan hollered from above.

"Yes. It's me."

"Are you alone?"

"Yes."

"I'm upstairs, come on in … oh, but wait, can you please take off your shoes."

Of course she wasn't going to wear shoes in Adeline's home. What an odd thing for Lan to say. Suzanne chalked it up to grief. The poor girl wasn't thinking straight.

Suzanne's hip was aching halfway up the first flight of stairs. It would be sore for several days now. She'd have to ice it when she got home.

As she stood on the second floor and relaxed for a quick moment, Suzanne peered back down into the main level. There wasn't a single Christmas decoration set up. Adeline was never one for overdoing it; still she usually had a few decorations displayed shortly after Halloween.

By the time Suzanne reached the third floor, she was silently cursing the building's architect. But those thoughts were quickly replaced. She was shocked by the bedlam within Adeline's bedroom. It was like in the movies when the bad guys tore a room apart looking for something. All the drawers, the closets, and even the mattress were askew. A sobbing Lan sat in the centre of the storm, her eyes were red and swollen. It was the first time that Suzanne had ever seen her without make-up. Three dresses were laid out upon the un-made bed.

"Jei Jei planned everything," Lan explained.

"Even the funeral arrangements. All except for one simple detail. The funeral director asked me how she'd like to be dressed. I didn't know what to say. I don't know what to do."

Such a trivial matter, but under such circumstances, Suzanne opted to treat Lan gently. "She always liked the colour purple."

"You don't think it's too much?" Lan wiped away her tears with her sleeve.

"Not for Adeline. Besides, the dress is no doubt from a designer label and cost more than Charles's car," Suzanne said, laughing, hoping a little levity would help soothe the situation.

Lan started crying again, and Suzanne didn't know what to say. So she sat down beside her friend and put her arm around her.

"I guess this is your home now," Suzanne said, the realization just hitting her. "Good luck with those stairs," she added.

"I could never live here. It's Adeline's place. She's everywhere. I never noticed how many pictures she took of herself." The walls were adorned with travel photos. Adeline had journeyed all over the world. In her bedroom alone were pictures from Paris, Milan, Macau, Atlantic City and what looked like Bali, but Suzanne couldn't be sure. Many of the older photographs were cut in half, which had been

Adeline's method of erasing any trace of her ex-husband from her fond memories.

"Did you ever travel with her?"

"Yes. Of course, I did," Lan answered. Her eyes skimmed the room and settled on what she must have been looking for. "See there on the far wall. That's us in Las Vegas four years ago. Back when I was still gambling of course. I lost a small fortune, and Adeline bought just about every designer purse that she could find. That place was just wicked for people like her and me...but oh, we had such a ball."

Suzanne would never set foot in a city like Las Vegas. Being surrounded by large crowds of drunken buffoons was pretty much the opposite of a fun vacation. She and Charles much preferred travelling within their adopted province. Still, she could see why Lan and Adeline would have had a good time together in sin city. Adeline had always acted demure, but it was painfully obvious why she chose the company of such a young friend. The vibrant Lan made her feel young and wild. She often wondered what Adeline's younger version would have been like. Scanning her bedroom, Adeline's possessions strewn on the floor gave Suzanne a tiny glimpse. "I can't imagine Adeline ever wearing that," she said, her eyes pointing towards a red boa.

"I remember that night like it was last week. But it was more like fifteen years ago. I found it in the back of her closet, and I'm shocked that she still had it. She wore it for a Vicars and Tarts party."

Suzanne really didn't want to walk down this particular path of memory lane with Lan. Adeline's distant past probably didn't have any relevance to her demise, Suzanne tactfully changed the subject, deciding to play a hunch, "You weren't in here just looking for a dress. It looks like you were searching for something."

"Ah, it's nothing."

"If it were nothing, you wouldn't have thrown her possessions everywhere." That came out way too patronizing. Suzanne didn't want to spook Lan, for she was liable to start crying again. So she dialled down her tone. "Come on, maybe I can help you find it."

Lan took a moment before saying, "You know that Adeline and Murray were once engaged, right?"

"I thought that he had asked her and she declined."

"That's not exactly true," Lan said sheepishly.

Suzanne sensed that Lan wanted to tell her something, but for whatever reason, she was hesitant. She decided to softly prod her grieving friend, "It's alright dear, you can tell me anything.

I'm all ears. It'll help if you talk about these things."

"It's a long story, I'm afraid."

"I love long stories," Suzanne said, as she eased herself free of Lan's embrace.

"Well, you see she knew that Murray once had money. After his car accident..." Lan's words stumbled. Suzanne didn't know why. She remained silent, patiently waiting for Lan to regain her composure.

"Well, after the accident, he was never the same. It wrecked his right knee and left him...a little simple in the head. You know about his accident, right?"

"Yes, I've heard about it," Suzanne nodded, not wanting Lan to dwell on Murray when she wanted to learn about Adeline.

"It happened before I knew him, but this is a small town, and we all knew about the accident. He was only twenty-two at the time and a shell of his former self. The insurance company, ICBC, determined that he wasn't at fault and they paid him a tiny fortune. But it wasn't enough to make him happy again. I guess no amount of money could ever be enough for what he was going through. He used to play hockey religiously. Some people say he could have played in the NHL, but all that was over now.

"He left Sechelt for a worldwide cruise, I guess just to get away from here," Lan continued. "No one heard from him for a while, but word got out that he had married a wealthy, older woman. I can't quite recall her name. What was it? Melissa, maybe... I don't know. Either way, they travelled the globe and lived it up. Wine and roses, that sort of thing. Well, after several very decadent years she passed away. It was rather sudden, in what some described as mysterious circumstances."

All this was news to Suzanne, and she listened in silence. She hadn't intended to be drawn into Murray's story.

"Well, Murray returned to Sechelt, and he bought a bunch of land and built a little cabin that he still lives in now. It was pretty much all anyone could talk about. Like I said, this used to be a much smaller town back then. Everyone knew everyone and folks didn't have all that much to talk about. Can you imagine? It was the return of Murray Wilthe and his perpetual reversal of fortunes. He was broken in both heart and body. That's when we met... through a mutual friend. Despite his unhappiness, he was a decent man. He still is. To his core, Murray is a good person. But I saw him over the years as he turned to drink and sank deeper and deeper into depression. That is until many years later when I introduced him to Adeline.

"It wasn't designed to be a setup. I never fathomed that there would be any romantic feelings between the two of them. I mean, Adeline was almost twenty years older than him. But I guess that's what Murray went for and shockingly, she was smitten with him. Still, she suspected that he had ulterior motives, and she wasn't about to be taken as a fool. She assumed that he dated older women for their money.

"She wasn't the least bit surprised when he proposed to her; she had seen it coming. She surmised that Murray must have spent all his money and was now looking for a new sugar mama. But then he gave her this amazing ring. It must have been at least two carats and shined like the moonlight on the ocean."

Lan paused, probably for dramatic effect, and Suzanne didn't interrupt her.

"Adeline must have been floored, so she inquired about his finances. Murray explained that he wasn't as poor at all. It was quite the opposite. He had saved pretty much every penny from his inheritance of his departed wife. He was still living off the settlement from the insurance company. If Murray wasn't trying to marry Adeline for her money, then he must genuinely have loved her. She said yes.

"Adeline was so happy," Lan explained. She rested and looked down before continuing. "But then something changed in her. A few days after the engagement, she called everything off. She never explained why, but she insisted that she couldn't marry him. She hinted once that she feared she'd end up like his first wife, but I didn't really believe it."

Suzanne was enthralled with the story. How had she never heard of this before? She had so many questions. "Why do you think she broke it off?"

"Did Adeline ever tell you of her vow to never to marry again after Anthony?"

"Yes, she told me once. She said she would never love a man again."

Lan smiled. "She told everyone that. But she loved Murray plenty. No, she vowed to never marry again, because it would mean that Anthony could stop paying her alimony."

"What?" Suzanne couldn't believe it. "Adeline wasn't like that."

"Adeline was a lot of things. Plus, you have to remember that Adeline was also a devoted Catholic. No sex before marriage, that kind of thing. It's preposterous if you ask me. Where's the fun in that?" Lan must have recalled her audience. "Oh wait... sorry, I didn't mean any offence."

"Please go on."

"Well, the relationship was done, it couldn't go anywhere. So Adeline tried to do the right thing and return the ring, but he insisted that she keep it."

"When did this all happen?" Suzanne asked.

"I don't know, maybe twelve years ago."

"And that's what you're looking for now, the ring?" Suzanne hid any trace of accusation in her voice. Of course, Lan wanted to find the ring. It was a small treasure and would be part of her inheritance.

"Yes," Lan blushingly admitted. "All her other jewelry is here."

"Maybe she had it in a safety deposit box?"

"No, that's not her style. Adeline was old school and didn't trust banks."

"A ring like that would have been insured," Suzanne said. "Maybe they know its whereabouts."

"No, Adeline hated insurance companies almost as much banks," Lan said, her voice completely dejected.

"She didn't hate them that much." Suzanne was a little puzzled. "Did you know that Adeline had a life insurance policy?"

"Really," Lan said, sounding very surprised.

"It was made out to Murray, and I hear that it was quite substantial."

"*Aiya!*" Lan said. It was all she said. Suzanne knew it to be a Cantonese expression of disappointment and frustration. It wasn't quite swearing, but close to it. Under these circumstances, Suzanne let it slide.

Suzanne stayed and helped look for the ring. She cleaned as she searched. The two friends talked, but mostly Lan rambled and sulked. She was in a dark place. Suzanne did her best to calm Lan down, but after thirty minutes, she knew that it was hopeless. It was almost four PM, tea time. She wanted to be home. She said, "I best get home and cook Charles his dinner. You know how he gets when he's hungry."

Chapter

6

Late afternoon

Suzanne returned to find a deserted home; her husband and dog were missing. She quickly assumed what had happened. After she left, Nero must have sat by the door and moaned. Inebriated or not, Charles couldn't stand hearing his dog unhappy. He would've taken his beloved pooch for a walk. He was probably upset that she hadn't taken Nero with her. Charles was the type of man who let things fester for a long time until he can't take it anymore. He's like a teapot that only on occasion blows its top. Undoubtedly, Charles wouldn't consider now as the proper time to get mad. He'd save it for later. Hopefully, all would be forgiven once she revealed to him everything she had uncovered.

She did the dishes and tidied the house as a form of penance that would surely appease him a little. The rain returned with a vengeance and Suzanne spotted Charles's umbrella by the door. Oh dear, that's not going to help the situation. She turned on the kettle and waited for him.

Soon after, the door opened, and Nero ran to her.

"My floors!" she hollered. "Dry his feet."

"Nero, come back here, boy."

She greeted Charles at the door, a towel in her hand. With a painful groan, she bent over and attempted to dry the drenched bulldog.

"Don't push yourself," her caring husband said without an ounce of malice. "Watch your hip. Let me do it."

"Thank you."

Charles was soaked through, but still he thoroughly dried Nero before thinking of himself. Suzanne took his wet jacket and sweater and returned with his housecoat.

"Where were you off to?" he asked as he slid into his slippers.

"I had to go see Lan. She was at Adeline's."

"Tidying up the place?" he asked.

"Quite the opposite," Suzanne said. "She's tearing the place apart looking for Adeline's engagement ring from Murray. I helped her for a while, but we couldn't find it."

"Adeline kept his ring?"

"Apparently so," Suzanne said. "Did Murray

ever discuss with you his feelings for Adeline."

"No. I sensed that he didn't want to talk about it. I could tell by the way he looked at her that he was still very much in love with her. Sad really. Anyways, I'm sure the ring will turn up. Knowing Adeline, it's probably tucked away in a sock drawer."

Suzanne brought their tea into the living room and sat down in her chair. Charles put his feet up on the couch, and Nero jumped onto his lap. "So, how's Lan coping?" he asked.

"Alright, I guess. She's a lot better today. But she was genuinely shocked to hear about the life insurance. She said that Adeline had been very clear with her that she was going to get everything. So this insurance policy paid out to Murray completely floored her."

"Still, Adeline must have been worth a fortune. I'm sure Lan is going to be just fine," Charles said.

"Not as good as we had initially thought. Lan told me that Adeline had re-mortgaged the townhome and the Mercedes is on a lease."

"Wow, I thought she was much wealthier."

"Me too," Suzanne admitted. "She was pretty much living from one alimony cheque to the next. Her affluence was a well-constructed façade."

They remained silent together, both

pondering why someone would go to such lengths merely to impress one's peers. Charles was the first to speak, "I had an interesting conversation with someone I met today too."

"Really, who was it?"

"Oh, don't worry about it." Charles liked to kid his wife; it was his version of fun.

"Come on, tell me." Suzanne liked to appease him by making it appear like it bothered her. She picked up her needlepoint and settled in.

Charles played coy for a while before finally announcing, "I had a nice talk with Byron."

"The Lord Byron himself graced you with his company?"

"Oh, I wish you'd stop talking about Byron that way. He's really a nice chap."

"If you say so," Suzanne said. "But his choice in women is very questionable."

"Love is blind," Charles said.

What an odd thing for him to say. Suzanne knew that Charles despised Regina almost as much as she did. Regina often hurt him as a way of punishing her. She remembered how just last year Regina had tried to have all pets banned. Strata rules required a three-quarter vote at the annual meeting for such a drastic change. But Regina didn't care about rules. Even though she didn't have the authority to revise the strata bylaws, she posted the new amendment in the monthly minutes. Shockingly very few people opposed her. Many of the residents didn't have pets, so they didn't care either way.

The next strata meeting was an all-out war. Mild-mannered Charles had one of those tea-boiling-over moments and Suzanne worried that he'd get violent. She had to escort him home and relied on Adeline to resolve the issue.

Later that night, Adeline visited them to report a compromise. Strata council agreed that all existing pets were allowed to remain, but new pets were not permitted. The proposed by-law would be voted appropriately upon in the upcoming annual meeting. Suzanne was still furious. There shouldn't have been any sort of compromise whatsoever. Regina wasn't following procedures. Where did she get off changing strata rules so arbitrarily?

Suzanne and Charles had to rile up their neighbours and ensure that they would be present at the next meeting. Luckily, Regina couldn't muster up enough votes to evoke the controversial by-law. Regina proposed that new rules shouldn't have to pass with such a restrictive quorum. That proposal was quickly dismissed by Suzanne and everyone else present. It was a rare political victory for Suzanne against her antagonist.

"Well, what did Byron have to say for himself?" Suzanne asked.

"That he had been sick with a nasty cold and that Regina had been staying at home to care for him."

"That's convenient."

"How's that?"

"Let me guess, he was home all day Sunday. He didn't go out for his weekly bird hike, but rather was in bed and Regina was there the whole time to tend to him."

"I don't know. I didn't ask him for specifics," Charles said defensively.

"You can bet the police would have asked him to give a detailed account of his whereabouts on Sunday. Or more precisely, his wife's."

"Ahh, I see," Charles clued in. "You think that he's lying to give Regina an alibi."

"It's pretty obvious."

"I don't know. He came to the door last week to campaign for Regina. He sounded like he was coming down with something."

"Whoa, back up the train, Byron came here to campaign for Regina. Who was he kidding?" She put down her needlepoint as she needed to fully concentrate on this conversation.

"I don't know. He was talking to everyone. I guess he just popped by here to say hi."

"When did he come?" Suzanne asked.

"Last Wednesday, while you were at Mahjong,"

"Why didn't you tell me this earlier?"

"It wasn't really relevant at the time. It's still not that important." Charles looked distressed. He didn't like being grilled.

"Alright then, what else did he have to say?"

"Are we talking about Wednesday or just now?" Charles sounded more and more flustered. He stirred in his chair, which caused Nero to get up and leave, but not before giving both his human parents the stink eye.

"Now, dear, stick with today," Suzanne said.

"He asked if you were thinking of running against Regina."

"Never again," Suzanne said.

"That's what I assured him," Charles said. "And he pointed out that since no one was running against her, the elections should be cancelled."

"There still has to be elections at the annual general meeting. What about the other seats? Betty and Yosef are running for council. Maybe now they'll make a bid for president?"

"They were only there for Adeline. Neither one of them has the inclination to be anything more than on council. And now that Regina stands un-opposed to remain president, they have both dropped out. They don't want anything to do with Regina."

"I swear this is all her doing." She stopped herself there. It was too early for her to publicly admit her suspicion of Regina, even to Charles. At least not until she could uncover a little more proof.

"What are you going to do about it then?"

"Whatever I can do." It wasn't time to be making a grand pledge, but inwardly she did promise herself that she was going to solve the murder of her dearest friend.

Charles finished his tea and offered to make more.

"No, thank you."

"Alright then, I'm off to bed." He rose and gave her three quick pecks on the check.

"Don't be ridiculous, we didn't have supper yet." Come to think of it, she hadn't even eaten lunch. Stress made her lose her appetite. Charles had probably eaten at The Dockside, and he was clearly still feeling the effects of his overindulgence. He was halfway up the stairs, when she called out, "Oh, I spoke to Caroline. I agreed that we'd go to see Dad this Christmas."

"Is Mark paying for it?"

"Yes."

"Then it'll be a holly jolly Merry Christmas after all. Goodnight, sweetie, I'll see you in bed."

****

Suzanne found herself alone in the dark again, only vaguely sensing the symptoms of skipping two meals. Her hands were busy with her needlepoint, functioning on auto-pilot, while her mind was occupied reviewing every conversation she'd had today. She completely ignored the telephone ringing beside her. A few moments later she heard a somewhat irate and groggy Charles call out from upstairs, "Pick up the phone Suzanne, it's Lisa."

She lifted the phone to her ear and heard, "I'll talk to you later, Pop."

He didn't respond. Charles was probably already halfway asleep again.

"Hello Lisa," Suzanne said into the phone. She placed her needlepoint down beside her.

"You agreed to go to Montreal for Christmas. I'm so excited."

"Yes, we're both looking forward to it," Suzanne said, mustering up as much enthusiasm as she could.

"Look, I know that you don't like Mark and me paying for everything. But it's not a big deal."

"It's not that it's not okay. It's just that, well, you know how your father gets. He's a proud man," Suzanne said.

Suzanne often used Charles as a scapegoat for her true feelings. She was aware that Lisa knew this little detail about her. Still, mother and daughter went through the routine of blaming Charles for any disagreement they had. They both knew that Charles was an easygoing man who wouldn't mind flying back to Montreal every month, as long as someone else was paying for it. Suzanne was the proud one who didn't like admitting that travelling during high season was out of their means.

"Thank you for convincing Dad. Grandpa is getting old. This could be his last Christmas," Lisa said.

"That's what you said last year."

"It was true then, just as it is now. Grandpa isn't getting any younger."

"None of us are, dear," Suzanne said. She and Charles had just travelled home to see her father on his birthday in September. Air travel after Labour Day was far more reasonable and Suzanne always liked the East in autumn. The trees were so beautiful as their leaves were turning colour and the temperature was just right.

"Well, I bought the tickets as soon as Caroline called and said that you had agreed. I booked us all on a flight for the eighteenth," Lisa said.

Suzanne was a little perturbed that her daughter had not consulted with her as to the departure date. It was just like Lisa to be so presumptuous. She decided to let it slide. "How long will we be staying?"

"Two weeks," Lisa said. "The boys are so excited."

Suzanne had always wanted to have boys but was instead blessed with two daughters. When her two grandsons were born, within a year of each other, Suzanne had a difficult time concealing her envy. But as the babies grew into toddlers her jealousy subsided. Her coveted bundles of joy transformed into two little balls of pure energy. They bounced off every wall and left snot under the furniture. Suzanne counted her lucky stars that God had given her girls.

After hanging up the phone, Suzanne realized that Lisa hadn't offered her any condolences. She wasn't offended. It was Lisa's way. She never liked talking about anything even remotely sad.

Suzanne closed her eyes and pictured her daughters as little girls again.

Caroline had been born a tomboy and was always closest to her father. She was always coming home with torn jeans and dirt on her face. She was as tough as nails and a star athlete in high school. It didn't come as a surprise to her when Caroline joined the army and later the Vancouver Police Department.

Lisa, on the other hand, had been their scholar. There had been a time when her relationship with her eldest daughter was unbreakable. They were as thick as thieves. Lisa was always getting excellent grades, collecting rocks and reading books. Suzanne's father had once said that Lisa often reminded him of her when she was a little girl. "Good luck," he had said.

Suzanne had known precisely what he was referring to. Along with Suzanne's intelligence, Lisa had also inherited her temperament and stubbornness. As little Lisa grew older, this led to a couple of long-term disagreements.

Their first significant row occurred when Lisa dropped out of UBC law in her third year because she was marrying Mark, a young lawyer with old money. She moved to the British Properties, a posh neighbourhood in West Vancouver, and slid into the role of a loyal housewife.

Suzanne argued that she should at least finish school. Lisa disagreed, saying, "What would be the point?"

Charles stayed out of it. He had been postponing his retirement in order to pay for Lisa's tuition. He wasn't disappointed with her decision and was happy for her. As her father, Charles would support her no matter what she did. And then he promptly retired.

"You and Lisa need a little space," Charles had said when he proposed that they sell their Vancouver home. They didn't need such a big house now that their two girls had moved out. "You have to let her live her life."

They sold their home and moved to the Sunshine Coast. "Still close, but not too close," Charles had said about the distance from West Vancouver to Halfmoon Bay.

Still close, but not too close, was also how Suzanne now felt about her relationship with her eldest child. She hid her displeasure as best as she could, but she knew that it was seeping out of her. She had always been convinced that her daughter was destined to be a great lawyer. Lisa was throwing away the potential of a gratifying career. Their disagreement festered until Isaac was born, and the two of them stopped fighting.

Suzanne had remained silent when Lisa opted not to baptize her children. She feared that her daughter was condemning the souls of her grandsons, but still she held her tongue. She knew that times were changing, and religion was becoming less and less critical in the lives of the young ones, even more so with the privileged youth who had no real motivation to pray.

Everything had remained reasonably calm until Lisa decided not to vaccinate her children. She had read somewhere on the internet that it had severe side effects. She tried to convince her mother to read the same website and, in the end, said that it was her decision on how to raise her own children. Suzanne resorted to something she didn't want to do. She spoke to Mark.

Suzanne had mixed feelings about Mark. He always worked long hours and had pretty much left the child-rearing to his wife. Suzanne called him and appealed to his logical side. She convinced him that for his sons' sake, he had to intervene.

A month later, Isaac and Thomas were vaccinated, but Lisa couldn't forgive her for involving Mark and turning him against her. It wasn't the kind of anger that would tear the two of them apart, but it was always there.

Lisa often sought her subtle revenge by flaunting her wealth. What better way than to fly the whole family home for the holidays, again. How could Suzanne refuse? She didn't like her daughter's motives, but Lisa was right. Papa wasn't getting any younger. This Christmas could very likely be his last.

Chapter

7

Sunday, December 6th, mid-day

Adeline Wong's funeral ceremony was a solemn affair. Suzanne noticed Father O'Brian's hands shaking throughout the service. She was suffering too. She couldn't hold back her tears as Lan gave her eulogy. Everyone cried.

After the speech, Lan went back to her seat beside Suzanne and whispered, "Are you going to say anything?"

Suzanne had written a few notes on a piece of paper, but she had just changed her mind. "You said everything that needs to be said, dear. It was beautiful."

"Thank you."

Suzanne leaned in closer and asked, "Is Adeline's sister here? I'd like to meet her."

"No, she couldn't make it."

At the reception, the Ricksons were seated at a table with two other couples: Ivan and Connie, and Adeline's neighbours, Walter and Dariya Underhill. They were swapping anecdotes and remembering Adeline fondly.

"I was shocked to see Anthony at the ceremony," Charles remarked. He looked uncomfortable in his suit. He had undone his top button and loosened his tie as soon as the service was over.

"I'm not," Suzanne said.

"I think he's sweet on Lanny," Connie smirked. Her hair was up in a bun, and she looked tired.

"Do you really think that Adeline's dearest friend is having an affair with her ex-husband?" Suzanne asked. "Connie dear, you see scandal everywhere."

Connie laughed. "True. In fact, I see scandal right now. Look by the food table." They all turned. "Who's that standing next to the honourable Lanny? Why, it's the devil himself, Anthony Wong."

"Wow, that's Tony?" Dariya pointed to him with her fork. "Walter and I were having brunch at Pebbles a couple of weeks ago, and we saw them there."

Connie's grin became so large it barely fit on her face.

"You saw them together before?" Suzanne turned her gaze to Walter, looking for a second witness.

"Yeah, pretty sure that was the guy." Walter nodded. "He's a right dandy Chinaman."

"Don't mind him. What my husband meant to say was that he dresses well." Dariya looked perturbed. Perhaps it was due to her husband's blatant racism, but Suzanne surmised that it was because she had sought Walter's confirmation of her story. Fair enough. Even on the best of days, Walter wouldn't have been a reliable source. The man had been pickling his liver for years, and his sight was far from dependable. Still, Dariya must be feeling pretty smug right now. She was the type of person that strived for attention. A nugget of surreptitious information must have been like a pocket full of gold. She often called herself the Rumour Queen of Secret Cove.

"Why didn't you ever tell us this before?" Connie asked.

Dariya smiled as she answered, "Because I didn't know who he was at the time. I was just happy that Lanny had found somebody new. She's a pretty girl and deserves to have a handsome suitor. Oh, and he drove her to the restaurant in this little blue BMW. So that makes him rich as well as handsome."

"I'm sure that Lanny would never date Anthony. She wouldn't do that to Adeline," Suzanne said.

"Well, they're up to something." Connie's grin wasn't fading. "Why else would they drive all the way out to Sechelt, instead of meeting at the Dockside or the Halfmoon Bay Cafe?"

The men were sitting quiet and looking restless. "They're up to it again," Ivan said.

"Gossiping like old hens." Walter rolled his eyes.

Charles waved to the bar. "Come on, let's get ourselves another drink."

"Good old Adeline," Ivan said. "She pre-arranged her own funeral service and threw in an open bar, even though she never touched a drop of alcohol in her life."

"It would be ungrateful of us not to accept her generosity." Walter laughed.

Suzanne scoffed at the comment. She had spotted him earlier drinking from a flask that had been concealed in his coat pocket. He'd probably already drained it and was now yearning for another drink. Curse him. Adeline may have arranged every detail of this lavish ceremony, but it was Lan who was paying for it now. Adeline had left very little money in her estate. No doubt this funeral service was draining whatever pittance was left.

As the men departed, the women continued their conversation without missing a beat. "Regardless of what they are up to, it's not right. Lan cavorting with Tony at Adeline's funeral no less," Dariya said.

"I'm sure it's nothing," Suzanne said. She wasn't sure of it, but she didn't want to stir the pot on today of all days.

"Look," Connie said. "Tony is leaving, and Lanny is chatting to someone else now. Let's go talk to him and ask him what's up with him and Lanny. My money is that they are lovers and have been for years."

"Count me out. I couldn't care less." Dariya stayed seated.

Connie and Suzanne glared at her.

"Alright," Dariya admitted. "My back hurts, and I don't want to move right now. Go talk to Tony and tell me everything he says."

"I guess it's the only way to find out for sure." Suzanne got up and left her cane at the table. Along with Connie, she went to intercept Anthony before he could make his getaway. An explanation was definitely required.

"Mrs. Rickson and Mrs. Heslop, it's a pleasure to finally meet you. Of course, I wish it was on better circumstances." Anthony said with a smile. His eyes were bloodshot, and he looked as though he'd been crying for days. He avoided making direct eye contact with Suzanne, and his gaze slipped to the main entrance. Despite his kind words, it was clear that he didn't want to be there any longer than he needed to be.

"Mr. Wong," Connie said. "I have to admit, we're very surprised to see you here."

"Please, call me Tony," he replied. "And to answer your question, Adeline was a very dear friend of mine. Despite our failed marriage and any illusion that my ex-wife may have maintained, we buried the hatchet several years ago."

"Really," Connie said, not concealing an ounce of her suspicion.

"That's nice to hear, Tony," Suzanne said. "I'm happy that you and Adeline were able to find peace before..." She stopped herself. She just couldn't say it.

"Well, I don't buy it," Connie went on. "So then, what's up with you and Lan? People have seen you two sneaking about together."

The directness appeared to take Anthony off guard. He hesitated before saying, "I'm sorry, that I can't tell you. You'll have to ask Lan about it. But please not now, she's not ready to talk about it. Give her some time."

It was clear that Connie didn't like the answer, "That sounds convenient for you. Does your wife know that you're here? I bet she doesn't."

"I never bet on anything," Tony said with conviction. "But I can assure you Carmen is home with the boys and fully aware of where I am. But I promised not to stay long. So on that note, I'll wish you both farewell, and my deepest condolences."

"I offer you mine as well, Anthony," Suzanne said, while Connie stood aghast.

Connie often bragged about her ability to rub people the wrong way. She had a tendency of never holding her tongue and always speaking her mind. She could do this because her mind was already made up regarding most things. "Come on Suzanne, you can't tell me that you believed a single word that scoundrel said," she proclaimed, on their way back to their table. Their husbands, along with fresh drinks, had already returned.

"He knew who we were," Suzanne said.

"What? That doesn't mean anything. Lanny could've told him."

"No, he's seen photos of us and seemed to know exactly who we are. Regardless of the nature of Lan's relationship with him, she wouldn't have shown him our pictures and told him our surnames. Adeline must have sat down with him and spoken fondly of us."

"I don't buy it," Connie insisted.

"I'd suspected before that Adeline had reconciled with her ex-husband. She was just too proud to ever admit it to us."

"Poppycock."

"It must have been Anthony who reviewed the strata accounts and exonerated Adeline of mismanaging the funds. He's a very reputable accountant, and even Regina wouldn't rebut his expertise. Who else could have reviewed the books?"

Connie seemed to concede that point. She too must have wondered about the identity of Adeline's secret auditor. All the pieces fit.

"So did you girls find what you were looking for," Ivan asked.

"Yes, honey," Connie said and went on to review their conversation with Tony and Suzanne's deductions about it.

"Wow, that's interesting," Charles said. "Do you know who else is here that you might find interesting?"

"Who?" she asked as she scanned the room to discover it herself.

"That young police fellow," Ivan blurted out.

"Really." Dariya looked about to find him too.

"My wife fancies the young officer and does little to hide it," Walter said to the table, before addressing Dariya directly. "Don't get too excited, sugarplum. He's going from table to table and talking to everyone. No doubt that he's on the clock and looking for one of us to slip up."

****

"Bonjour, my friends," Staff Sergeant Laval said. "Do you mind if I have a seat?"

It had taken him over twenty minutes to make his way to their table. The men had time to finish their drinks and head to the bar for more while the women continued to speculate about Anthony.

"Please do." Dariya offered him Walter's vacant seat. "My husband won't be back for a while. He seemed very eager to chat up Miss Wilson."

"Oh, you're such a jealous little mouse, Dariya." Connie snickered. "Walter's so drunk he's probably in the bathroom, having a polite conversation with the toilet bowl."

"My Walter can hold his liquor." Dariya's cheeks were turning red.

"I hear that it was a lovely service," Laval said. "Did any of you give a eulogy?"

"No," Suzanne answered. Laval was clearly not here to listen to them argue. He wanted information from them, and with any luck, maybe she'd learn a thing or two also. "Lan gave a beautiful speech, and no one wanted to go after her."

"Suzanne was going to go, but she chickened out," Charles said jokingly.

"I didn't chicken out of anything. It's just that Lan had said pretty much everything that I had written. It would have been repetitive."

"Bok bok," Dariya clucked and flapped her arms.

Suzanne glared at her. Equally upset with her husband for starting it.

"So, have you come to haul away our dear Suzanne," Ivan asked.

"Don't joke." Connie reprimanded her husband.

Suzanne was not amused. She took a long breath.

"No, Mr. Heslop, I'm not here today to make any arrests. I'm merely here to pay my respects." Laval's eyes darted from person to person.

"Don't be coy, Staff Sergeant," Ivan said. "You never met Adeline. You're here to examine us. Watch our every move and see if someone seems out of place. You believe that Adeline's killer is in this room now."

"It's a possibility but not a certainty, Mr. Heslop," Laval said. "And yes, I am here to observe."

"Well, you can stop looking. Tony Wong just left." Connie remarked. Clearly, all of Suzanne's rationalizations hadn't changed Connie's opinion of Adeline's cheating ex-husband.

Dariya was quick to jump on the bandwagon, "I've got my money on him being the killer too. He's been paying her alimony for over thirty years. He must be getting tired of financing her countless facelifts and vacations."

"Perhaps you would be surprised to know that in thirty-three years, Anthony Wong has never missed a payment and he's never late. In fact, we discovered seven dated cheques in Adeline Wong's desk. He was, by all accounts, the ideal ex-husband," Laval revealed.

This new information didn't surprise Suzanne, but she was astonished that Laval was so forthcoming about an active investigation.

Ivan jumped into the fray, "Were you ever able to catch up with Murray Wilthe?" he asked the detective.

"I can't say that we have. Have you had any better luck?"

"No one has seen him in days," Charles answered. He always liked Murray, but even he had to admit that the sudden disappearance was highly suspicious. Charles had been heading the search party to find his friend. Murray hadn't been to work or the pub since Wednesday. He did have a drinking problem, and it isn't uncommon for him to just disappear on a binge. "Murray wouldn't hurt a fly. So I don't believe he ever could have harmed Adeline. He loved her."

"Love can make us do crazy things," Ivan countered. "And unrequited love can drive any man insane."

"But it wasn't one-side, Adeline had that life insurance policy for him," Connie said.

"Ah, but he didn't know that." Ivan wagged his finger.

"How do you know?" Connie raised her voice.

Connie and Ivan were about to go at it again, oblivious to anyone else around them.

Laval interrupted them, "What about you, Ms. Rickson? Who's your prime suspect?"

Everyone else at the table answered in unison, "Regina Snow."

Suzanne hid her annoyance at being so easy to read. She could almost hear Adeline reminding her to keep her cards close to her chest. She felt as though everyone was picking on her, including Laval. "I'd like to point out that Regina didn't come to this funeral. No doubt she's at home, fraught with guilt."

"Byron was at the ceremony, and he was crying like a baby," Connie said.

"He's a very emotional man," Charles added.

"That's a very polite way of calling a man a sissy," Ivan laughed, spilling his drink.

"I'm surprised that Regina isn't here." No one had noticed Lan arrive at the table and insert herself into the conversation.

Suzanne looked up at her, "Why's that?" Lan appeared to be nervous and on edge. The bags around her eyes were expected. But she was fidgeting with her jade necklace with one hand, while the other hand was shaking. Maybe it was because she was watching what little she had of an inheritance trickling away as the bar bill grew, or perhaps it was something else.

"They really weren't enemies," Lan answered. "In fact, they were usually very civil to each other at strata meetings."

"Regina is like that. She always smiles to your face. But she also has a dagger poised for whenever you turn your back."

"You exaggerate Suzy. Regina is quite liked in the community. She can indeed be bossy and stubborn, but when you're the strata president, you sometimes have to ruffle a few feathers," Lan said.

Suzanne was dumbfounded. She hated being called Suzy. Regina often called her Suzy, just to be annoying. Why was Lan calling her that now? And why was she sticking up for Regina? Are they friends now? What was going on in this place? Perhaps the best way to find out would be to act normal. "What do you girls think about playing Mahjong again?"

"But who'd replace Adeline," Connie asked?

"No one could replace Adeline," Suzanne responded. "But obviously Dariya could take her spot. She's often our spare, so why not make her permanent? What do you think, Dariya?"

Dariya looked elated. It was no secret that she loved any opportunity to get out of her home. The thought of being a regular must have excited her beyond words. "I'd love that. Thank you," she said.

"Where would we play?" Lan asked and turned to Dariya. Clearly, she was implying that as the newest member, she should volunteer her home. But Dariya remained silent. Suzanne knew that even though Dariya didn't want to admit it, Walter would never allow four women milling about in his home twice a week.

"If you don't mind, Lanny dear, could we all play at Adeline's home," Suzanne asked. "It's the best option because our units are too small and cramped."

Lan's face revealed great trepidation. But as the three other women gazed at her, she eventually came around. "Why not," she said.

Good, Suzanne thought. If I can ease everyone back into a comfortable routine, maybe I'll be able to get a few straight answers out of them.

Chapter

8

Monday, December 7th, morning

Suzanne didn't get much sleep at night. She couldn't stop reviewing and replaying the events at the funeral. There were so many questions. So many possibilities and Lan seemed to be in the centre of the storm. Talking to Lan and uncovering any secrets she might be hiding was her number one priority.

Suzanne kept asking herself, how well do I know my friend? Much of what she knew about Lan had been from Adeline, who, in her own right, was proving not to be the most trustworthy of sources. But Adeline had been simple. Most of her lying wasn't really lying. It had been more like posturing. Adeline had once explained that it was part of her Asian culture to always maintain face. Lan, on the other hand, seemed different. Her motives were more complicated.

As far as Suzanne was aware, Lan had been born in mainland China, to upper-middle-class parents. They wanted the best for her, so they hired an English tutor from Canada named Henry. The two of them fell in love while Lan was still a teenager. It's unclear what horrified the parents more, the under-age sexual relationship or that their daughter was sleeping with a white man. Either way, her parents had Henry deported. But their plan backfired when he married Lan, and returned to Canada with his new bride in hand. As far as Suzanne knew, Lan had never spoken to her family again.

The young couple settled in Henry's hometown, Sechelt, and he found work in a lumber mill. Sadly, tragedy struck five years later when Henry was killed in a car crash along with their young daughter. Lan was in her early twenties, and she had lost everyone in her life. In grief counselling, she met Murray, and the two of them became fast friends. Eventually, Lan picked up her life and went back to school to study dental hygiene. She never married again.

Suzanne was woken by Nero running up the stairs and into her room. This behaviour was unheard of. The dog knew better than to wake her up too early in the morning. But then she noticed two things. Charles was not in bed, nor was it early. It was almost ten. She couldn't remember the last time that she had slept in that late. It was a well-needed repose. Last night's restlessness had been recurring over the past week.

"Rise and shine, sleepyhead. Breakfast is served." Charles was standing in the doorway. She could smell the scrambled eggs and bacon. Charles loved his bacon, but Suzanne rarely made it for him. She never touched the stuff because of her high blood pressure and didn't think it wise for her husband to over-indulge. Clearly, Charles had taken the initiative to treat himself today.

"Nero needs his walk," she said.

"Already done. Now get up and let's eat. I'm starving." Her faithful husband never ate breakfast without her.

"We need to pick up some flowers today," she said after her first bite of toast.

"We're going to visit Lanny?" he asked.

"Not we. I have a lot of questions for her, but she's still in a very fragile state. I don't want her to think that we're ganging up on her."

After breakfast, the Ricksons drove to the Halfmoon Bay General Store and bought a medium-sized bouquet. The store clerk remarked on how he had been selling lots of flowers of late. "Many early Christmas parties," he concluded.

Suzanne figured that noon was a reasonable time to call on Lan. She phoned first, but no one answered. With the bouquet in one hand and her cane in the other, she headed out to Adeline's.

The front door was unlocked. Suzanne found Lan sitting in the den, where they used to play Mahjong together. There was a glass of water on the table, and it looked as if Lan was nursing a hangover. No one could blame her if she'd gotten drunk last night. It must have been a long day for her. "Can I get you something?" Lan asked.

"I'll have some water too, but don't get up. I'll pour it myself."

Lan insisted on getting it herself. Years of being in the company of both Adeline and Suzanne had ingrained in her the same desire to be the perennial gracious hostess. She reappeared from the kitchen with a glass of iced water and some cookies. Despite her earlier intentions, she was making herself very much at home here. Suzanne said nothing of the subject. Instead, she very warmly asked, "Any luck finding the elusive ring?"

"None, but I haven't given up." Lan was relaxed, and the house was noticeably cleaner.

"It was a lovely service yesterday."

"Yes," Lan agreed. "But I fear I owe you an apology. I was a little out of my head."

"How so?" Suzanne was expecting an apology, but not so quickly. Still, she didn't want to let Lan off the hook too fast. An explanation was irrefutably required.

"I was stressed, I guess. I'm not myself. I realized later that I was making you look bad in front of that nice police officer. What's his name?"

"Staff Sergeant Laval," Suzanne answered. "And no, you weren't making me look bad."

"Well, let's say I was playing devil's advocate for your least favourite person. I'm sorry. But Regina has been accommodating of late. I know you think she did it, but she insists that she was with Byron all Sunday morning. Staff Sergeant Laval appears to believe her."

Suzanne noted that everyone agreed with her initial assessment: that the killer had snuck into Adeline's home while they were at church. This meant that no one thought that she had deliberately tainted the jam before giving it to Adeline. Maybe she wasn't a suspect after all. Even Regina had never outwardly accused her of being a murderer, but then again, that wasn't her style. Regina planted the seeds and let others come to their own conclusions. She never stuck her own neck out, and she never did her own dirty work.

Suzanne was slowly learning to do the same. "It wouldn't be prudent of me to accuse Regina of anything," she said. She needed to keep Lan relaxed and forthcoming. "But I do very much want to help the police solve this crime. And as such, I require your input and insight. I need you to tell me about your relationship with Anthony."

"I realize that it might look bad. But it's all a funny story really. Well, not at first, but it ends happily. You see, I knew about Tony of course. Adeline had told me so much about him, like how he left her after ten years of marriage. Poor Adeline couldn't have any children, and Tony always said that it was okay.

"But I guess it wasn't okay, because one day he tells her that his secretary, Carmen, is pregnant and that it's his child. Adeline was devastated. Well, as you know, they divorced, and Adeline faired quite well. He sent her pre-dated cheques, and they barely talked to each other for over thirty years. Amazing right?" Lan appeared a touch cheerier than before. Adeline had always been elusive about her relationship with Anthony and Lan was perhaps the only person she ever really spoke to. Lan seemed relieved to finally tell someone else the secrets she'd been keeping for decades.

"It stays that way, until one day, guess who walks into my dental office? You see, I knew him by name, but not by appearance. But there aren't that many Wongs on the Sunshine Coast not like the mainland. So I knew it was a strong possibility that it was the same Tony Wong. And you know me, I get to talking, and we hit it off. Not romantically, of course. He's a true gentleman, in every sense. He's extremely nice, easy to confide in and very attentive."

Lan looked up and hesitated. Their eyes locked, and Suzanne gestured for her to proceed. "Well anyways, Tony's gums are horrible. My boss, Dr. Ozeri, has Tony coming in for cleanings every three months. And guess who does all those cleanings? I tell Adeline everything of course, and she was cool with it all. But she didn't want me to reveal to Tony that I knew her…sorry, I'm rattling on, forgive me."

Suzanne waved her off, "No, please go on. It's all quite interesting."

Lan inhaled and continued. "Long story short, Tony and I became friends. He has two boys, both in university. He helps me out with my personal finances. The man's a genius. He's been doing my taxes for the last three years.

"I was keeping Adeline informed of everything, and one day she gets all Christian on me and says that it's time that she forgave Tony. I revealed this to Tony and set up a get-together for the two of them. I guess it went well. But as much as Adeline's a good Christian, she's still very much Chinese. She'd been mouthing off about Tony for dozens of years, and she didn't want anyone to know that she'd reconciled with him. I'm surprised that you, of all people, never figured it out."

"I had my suspicions," Suzanne confessed. "But I never said anything. Adeline's business was her own."

"Well, there you have it. I'm sorry that I kept it from you."

"It's alright. I understand."

Both women sat silently for a few moments. Suzanne wondered if he should be taken off of her suspect list, for he no longer had a valid reason to murder her. If Byron wasn't lying and Regina was really home with him all Sunday morning, then there's only one person left with the possible means and motive to harm Adeline. "Have you heard anything from Murray?" she asked.

"Not for a while," Lan said, her eyes darted away. Clearly, she didn't want to talk about it. After a short pause, she said, "I saw him after Adeline died. He reeked of alcohol. I thought he would be at the funeral, but I haven't seen him since."

"No one has," Suzanne remarked. She needed to ask Lan a question that she knew would rile her up. But still she had to ask, "I know Murray is your close friend, but do you think it's remotely possible that he had secretly learnt about the life insurance policy before Adeline's demise?"

"I don't think so." Lan rubbed her pendant. "Oh God, you think that Murray killed her? He'd never hurt anyone."

"You told me last week that his first wife may have died under mysterious circumstances."

"*Aiya*, that's just the kind of drama that Adeline liked to spout. I'm sure she died of cancer, or a heart attack, or something normal and mundane." Lan was on edge again.

"You said they were abroad when it happened." Suzanne started pushing, even though she knew that she shouldn't. "What if Murray was slowly poisoning her with arsenic? It's not like they would have performed an autopsy. If an older lady passed away in her sleep while on a cruise, no one would even blink an eye. It probably happens all the time."

"You think Murray killed his first wife for money and when he discovered that he was the beneficiary of Adeline's life insurance policy, he killed her too. You're absurd! I assure you Murray couldn't care less about money. He loved his wife, and he loved Adeline!"

Suzanne took a deep breath, "I don't think anything at this time. I'm sorry to have rattled you. I was just asking questions. I don't really know Murray all that well."

"Well, that's your loss. Ask your husband. Charles will tell you, Murray is a good man."

"I don't doubt that. But I do think that it's important that we find Murray soon. The police are looking to speak to him, and it doesn't look good that he's skipped town."

"Murray didn't leave town."

"How do you know that?" Had she just caught Lan in a lie?

"I... I don't know for sure. I just don't think he did." Lan stared at her feet.

"When did you say you saw him last?" Suzanne asked.

"I think it was a few days ago."

"Which day exactly?"

"I think it was Thursday."

"Thursday, are you sure?" Suzanne probed.

Lan took a moment to think. Suzanne wasn't sure if her friend was busy fabricating a lie or if she was sincerely ensuring the accurate date. Considering the events of the last week, Lan's perspective was probably blurred. "Yes, it was Thursday," she finally said. "Grey's Anatomy was on. Why? Does it matter?"

Sometimes Lan can be really daft, Suzanne thought. "Yes dear, it does. It makes you the last person to have seen him."

Chapter

9

Just before tea time

The phone rang, and Suzanne quickly answered. It was just the person she was hoping to hear from. Caroline skipped the pleasantries and got straight to business, "The lab results are in, and they have singled out your jam as being contaminated with *Convallaria majalis.* It's more commonly known as lily of the valley."

"See, I told you."

"This isn't one of those times that you should be bragging about being right, Mom."

"Well thank your friend for keeping us informed, and keep up the good work."

"I can't keep spying for you."

Suzanne was about to remind her daughter of the significance of every little piece of information required to clear her good name, but something caught her eye as she was peering out of her kitchen window. Two of the most unlikely people were walking up to her driveway. "I'll have to call you back, dear."

Regina Snow dressed like a politician. She kept her hair shoulder length and dyed a sandy auburn. Suzanne had never spotted a hint of grey on her. In a word, her fashion sense could be summed up as sharp. By contrast, Byron dressed as if every day was casual Friday at Value Village. He was clad in pleated khakis and a logo-less polo shirt. They marched in unison in a direct path to the Rickson's home. Byron was holding a large bouquet, too grand to be from the General Store and most likely purchased from a fancy Sechelt florist. As they reached the front door, Regina took the flowers from her husband so he could ring the doorbell.

"Who's there, dear?" Charles asked from upstairs. "Are you going to get it?"

"You should come down," she said. The two of them answered the door together.

Regina spoke first, "Our deepest condolences. Adeline was a good woman, and I always liked her very much. I'm going to miss her input at our strata meetings." She handed Suzanne the bouquet.

Instinctively, Suzanne bent her head to inhale the aroma of the fresh-cut flowers. Three long-stemmed white roses stood out from the rest. She was at a loss for words. Her mind was reeling. What was Regina up to?

"Thank you Byron and Regina, that's very kind of you both," Charles filled the silence. "We missed you at the funeral service."

"I didn't want to cause a scene. My presence would only have been a distraction," Regina explained.

"I went to the ceremony," Byron looked uncomfortable, but then again, he always looked that way.

"Yes, we saw you," Charles said. "Why didn't you come to the reception?"

"He didn't feel up to it," Regina said. "Look, Suzanne, I was hoping we could bury the hatchet. For Adeline's sake."

That was the second time she'd heard that expression in as many days. Anthony had used it the day before. She wondered if there was a connection between Regina and Anthony. Suzanne measured her words. "You started that outlandish rumour that Adeline was sleeping with Charles." Suzanne spoke in a relaxed manner. She wanted to scream, and it took every ounce of her willpower to remain civil. She reminded herself of Adeline's advice, play your cards close to your chest. "If you really want to bury the hatchet, admit to everyone about all the lies that you've spread."

"I agree with you," Regina said. "It's preposterous to think that your husband would ever stray from you. I can assure you that I would never sully myself by starting such a falsehood."

No, Regina would never own up to her wrongdoing. Suzanne decided on a different tact, "How about you step down as strata president? You know that you were going to lose. So postpone this election, withdraw your candidacy and let someone else step up."

"Someone like you?" Regina said snidely.

"No, not me. You have my word that I will never run again," Suzanne said.

"In the spirit of peace," Regina said, "I'll tell you why I've never been worried about this election. Because I've already won. Our neighbours are spineless and didn't want to get involved in a spat between Adeline and me. So I offered them an easy way out."

Regina paused. Charles leaned in closer. "What did you do?"

Regina smirked. "When Adeline had asked them to support her, almost everyone said yes, but only because they didn't want to be rude. I'd already spoken to them and asked them to sign proxy votes. That way, they could stay at home on election night and avoid having to chose sides in person."

Suzanne wanted to scream but stayed quiet. Charles spoke up, "But people must have been concerned that they were handing you the election."

"I told them that Adeline was doing this too and each of our collected proxy voters would even out. They bought it, and I knew no one would tell, because that would mean admitting they were gutless."

"You still need a majority of residents to attend the meeting to reach quorum," Charles said.

"Oh, I'm sure Adeline's supporters and a good many of mine would show up to the meeting. It would have been a tight race, but I'm confident my proxy votes would have nudged me to victory. I guess now we'll never know."

Suzanne clenched her fists so hard that her nails pierced her skin. The last comment twisted the dagger and stung more than the physical pain. Charles remained silent, utterly defeated. Even Byron seemed pale and surprised, perhaps because he had never imagined that his wife would be so forthcoming.

Charles took his wife's hand and gently squeezed it. It was a signal they'd established many years ago. Stop talking.

"Just go," Suzanne broke her silence. "And take your flowers."

"You keep them. Give them to Lanny if you like." Regina said. "Obviously you're upset, and I understand that. But remember, I only told you all of this because I want to be honest with you from now on. I promise you, no more deceiving, no more games. It's time for us to make peace, Suzanne."

Nero peeked through Suzanne's legs to see what all the commotion was about. Regina looked down at him with an air of disgust but then changed her expression to a grin. "Hello boy." She knelt down and tried to pat him.

He growled, and she jumped back.

"You have to let him smell you first, honey," Byron explained.

"Look, Nero here is getting restless. I have to take him for a long, overdue walk." Charles rubbed the back of his neck.

"Then we should be off." Byron took a step back from the door. Regina appeared less willing to depart.

"Wait," Suzanne said. "Before you go, can you tell me if your son was here last week?"

"No, he wasn't," Regina answered. "Why do you ask?"

"We saw his truck here, right up until last Saturday. It was parked in the last stall for several days. You know that long term visitor parking is not permitted."

Regina twitched, and Byron interjected, "I assure you, Noah wasn't here last week. It must have been someone else's truck."

The Snows walked away as Suzanne uttered to herself, "Like your word is worth anything."

Charles rolled his eyes. "Remember to breathe, dear."

"Of course I'm breathing. If I weren't breathing I'd be dead."

"I'm going to take Nero for his walk." Charles grabbed his coat.

"I'll come with you," she said. "I could use the fresh air."

Charles groaned, but she ignored it.

****

Suzanne considered tossing the flowers directly into the bin, but they were far too beautiful for such a fate. She cut a few inches off the bottom of the stems and placed them in her finest vase.

"Are you coming?" Charles asked impatiently from the front door, his boots and coat already on.

"Hold your horses."

"Nero and I will wait for you outside," Charles said. "And don't forget your cane."

The Ricksons slowly walked towards the coast, heading to the Secret Cove Marina. Suzanne didn't speak and grasped Charles's hand for comfort. She watched her dog stroll down the street. Nero's gait had significantly declined in the past year. He often paused to smell the earth and regain his stamina. This suited her perfectly, as she too enjoyed the constant breaks.

After her fall last year, Suzanne had been bedridden for several months. Recovery was slow, and she had to remain patient. She rarely came out for a walk anymore for her pace had deteriorated to the point that Charles often joked that she only had two speeds: dead slow and dead stop. There was no jesting today.

The fresh air soothed her petulance. All three of them took in the bright day and enjoyed the views of the Salish Sea and Echo Island.

They stopped once again as Nero had some business to attend to. Charles picked this moment to ask, "Why do you think Regina told us her plot to rig the strata vote?"

"Technically, she didn't rig it. Collecting the proxy votes was perfectly legal. I had anticipated her to cheat and spread rumours again. This wasn't a typical maneuver for her, which is probably why I didn't see it coming. It was unfair but impeccably legitimate."

"Regardless of its legitimacy, why tell us?" Charles asked as he scooped up Nero's business into a green, plastic bag.

"I was pondering the same thing," Suzanne admitted. "And all I can think is that she's telling the truth. Maybe she really does want to bury the hatchet between us. But why?"

"I already know what you're thinking. Regina is acting nicely in hopes that we don't suspect her of poisoning Adeline."

"Exactly," Suzanne said.

"Only you would consider someone's attempt at being nice and as a sign of guilt. But I have to admit, I trust Regina even less now too. Which baffles me, because she's not a dumb lady. She has to know that we'd see her actions as blatant and shady."

"Maybe we're reading too much into this, dear." In truth, she didn't want to be discussing this matter with Charles any further. He was often her sounding board, but first, she needed to think about it on her own. She needed quiet time to reflect. She wanted to concentrate on every minute detail before coming to conclusions. She'd discuss it with him later, and perhaps even with Caroline, whose experience with criminals would undoubtedly prove useful.

Hand in hand they remained. They walked past the marina and the Dockside Bar and Grill. Suzanne felt Charles' gentle tug towards his favourite pub, but she disregarded him. Silly man, she thought. We have Nero with us. Or is he hoping I'll wait outside with the dog?

Instead, they sat on a cold bench at the end of the dock. Together they took it all in.

Everything was calm and relaxing. Suzanne remembered why they had chosen to retire in Halfmoon Bay. The salty ocean air filled her lungs. Seagulls swooped down in search of clams, and a kingfisher sat atop a buoy. There were a dozen or so boats docked at the marina, but there wasn't a person in sight. It was all theirs and theirs alone.

It was the farthest that Suzanne had walked since her accident. She would be feeling the repercussions tomorrow or perhaps as soon as that evening. But for now, she felt compelled to enjoy the moment and bask in the sun. One never knows how long the sunshine will last.

Chapter

10

Tuesday, December 8th, late morning

"Could we come in and talk, Ms. Rickson?" Staff Sergeant Laval stood in the doorway, accompanied by an older officer of lesser rank. Both men stood up straight and tall, but the older man was a good five inches taller. Suzanne recognized him as the officer who had notified them of Adeline's demise at the hospital. What was his name again? It started with a 'B'. She scanned his face. Pleasant enough but his nose was a little flat. He'd probably played football in high school.

"Yes, of course." With a swift motion, Suzanne swung the door open wide, inviting both men inside. She regretted it instantly. The quick action had tweaked her hip. It had been sore all morning and was only getting worse.

Suzanne had anticipated the arrival of the police. Earlier in the day, she had visited Lan and Connie. The plan was to collect the jams herself and to mitigate any further scandal of the police going to her friends' homes. Luckily, she had only given this year's jam to her three friends, as she was awaiting their appraisal before handing them out to everyone. A small blessing, she figured. She couldn't imagine the upheaval if the police had to visit half the complex, going door-to-door, retrieving her jam from everyone. Even Suzanne, as thick-skinned as she was, couldn't bear such a humiliation. For the first time in a while, she felt ahead of the game.

"Allow me to introduce you to Corporal Bridges," Laval said, as the officer tipped his hat.

"We've met," the Ricksons said in unison.

"At the hospital," Bridges said. "I'm sorry it was under such sad circumstances."

Charles shook his hand, and Suzanne offered to make them some tea. The officers declined, but Suzanne put the kettle on anyway.

"I'm afraid that I only have troubling news," Laval said. "We found traces of a toxin in the jam that you gave Ms. Wong as a gift."

"I had a feeling that that was going to be the case. To make all of our lives easier, I took the liberty of retrieving the two other two jars I gave away as gifts. I have packed them up, along with the remainder batch for you. It's a little heavy I'm afraid, but two young, strapping men shouldn't have a problem lifting it." Suzanne said. She had been practicing these lines all morning.

Laval looked at her suspiciously. "Are you saying that you have already collected the jam from your friends?" he asked.

Laval was a bright man. It wouldn't have taken much digging to discover that Suzanne's daughter was the infamous Constable Rickson of the VPD. Her name was everywhere. He would assume that Caroline had tipped her off about the poison being in her jam. She had to protect her daughter. She had to act like nothing more than a sweet, old lady.

As innocently as she could, Suzanne responded, "I hope you don't mind, but I felt the urge to be prudent. By the way, my friends both have tasted their jams, and they said that it was delicious. And for the record, Lan and Connie are still very much alive."

Laval appeared to let it go, a fish to fry another day perhaps. "I'm afraid we came here today for more than just the jam. Tell me, Mr. and Ms. Rickson, have either of you visited the Sechelt Library recently?"

"I go sometimes," Charles blurted out.

"Define recently," Suzanne said.

"Within the last month," Laval answered.

"Yes," Charles said. "I sometimes go to use their computers as we don't have the internet here. I was there last week researching the poison that was used to murder Adeline."

"When was the last time before that?" Laval asked.

Charles thought for a moment. "I can't recall. It's been a while, longer than a month for sure."

When Laval turned his gaze to Suzanne, she responded, "I used to go regularly, years ago, but when the senior centre set up a book swap, I stopped using the library. I still visit Talewind Books in Sechelt from time to time, but I haven't been to the library in a long while." Suzanne caught herself rambling again. She always did when she was nervous. She tried to soothe herself and inhaled.

Laval kept his eys on Suzanne and said, "We received an anonymous tip that you had borrowed a book about household poisons."

"I did no such thing," Suzanne said, her calmness snuffed out.

"We'd like to have a look around, would that be alright with you?" Laval asked.

"Suit yourselves."

Laval seemed to sense her trepidation, "Let me ask you a question, Ms. Rickson, if you don't mind."

"I'm starting to mind. But go ahead and ask your question."

"If someone wanted to plant evidence against you, where do you think they'd leave it?"

Suzanne pondered the question before responding, "In plain sight."

"Hidden where it wouldn't look out of place, yet easily found," Laval said. "So where would you hide a book?"

"On a bookcase," Charles answered.

The Rickson's had a tall thin bookshelf in their living room. It was where Suzanne kept her favourite books. It all appeared flawlessly tidy. Every novel was sorted alphabetically by the author's surname. Laval must have noticed her collection of L.R. Wright novels because he jested, "I hope you're not comparing me to Staff Sergeant Karl Alberg?"

Suzanne chuckled. The joke managed to temporarily pacify her. "That depends, is your wife a librarian? Perhaps she is the anonymous tipster."

"I'm not married, Ms. Rickson."

Suzanne had already assumed that he was single, and she was happy to confirm it.

Together they continued to scan every title, looking for a book that did not belong.

"There," Charles pointed to the fourth shelf. Among the L's was a softcover book titled *A Beginner's Guide to Household Poisons* by Sam Ratchett. Suzanne had never felt more violated in her life. Not only had someone broken into their home, but they also rifled through her precious books.

"That's not ours," Charles said as he reached to grab it.

"Stop," Laval ordered as he produced a clear plastic bag from his pocket. "We need to check it for fingerprints. If you didn't take out the book and put it here…"

"Our prints won't be on it." It wasn't like Suzanne to cut someone off. She needed to sit.

"Have you noticed anything missing from your home?" Corporal Bridges asked.

"I don't know, let me think." Charles frowned. "Who would do this?"

"I'm afraid you're both going to have to come down to the station for us to take your fingerprints," Laval said. "You don't have to come right away, but I advise you to come soon," he added.

"We understand," Charles said. "And thank you for your courtesy. This has been very taxing on us both."

Suzanne was now mad at everything: the police officers in her home, the killer, and the predicament which they were putting her in. She wished that she could turn back the clock. The boiling kettle gave her an excuse to leave. Without a word, she retreated into the sanctuary of her kitchen. When her kids were younger, the family had a swear jar. She would have offered it a handsome donation.

She practiced her breathing techniques and did her best to calm down. She could get through this. She had to. She put on a smile and returned with a tray containing four cups of tea.

Staff Sergeant Laval was examining the book. "See here," he said. "There was once a label along the bottom of the spine. If it were recently removed, there would still be traces of the adhesive."

"Surely you don't think that we took out a book on poisons before killing Adeline," Charles asked.

"I learnt very early in my career, not to over-estimate criminals … but in your case, no. I don't think that you borrowed a book on poison right before murdering your friend. But somebody has devised an intricate scheme to make it appear as though you did."

"I trust that you see through it," Suzanne said. She was reasonably sure that Laval believed her, but she wasn't so sure of Corporal Bridges.

"I'll look into this, Mr. and Ms. Rickson," Laval said as he accepted a cup. "Our perpetrator seems to know your coming and goings, which makes me even more certain that the criminal lives among you in Secret Cove."

"I agree with you," Suzanne said.

Charles took a sip of hot green tea. It appeared to soothe him.

"Is there anywhere the two of you could stay for a short while?" Laval asked.

"Don't be ridiculous, I'm not leaving my home," Suzanne said.

Laval didn't argue with her. He has done his job by advising us to leave, Suzanne thought. It was up to them to pay heed to his warning or not. She worked out the details out in her head: if the killer had wanted to harm them, they could have done so already. This recent move was puzzling. The killer had been planning this scheme for quite some time. This was a brazen move, but essentially it had minimal effect. She knew that she had Laval to thank for that. A lesser mind may have arrested her already.

Laval straightened up and said, "I will contact you early tomorrow with any news I have. In the meantime, I would advise you to change your locks and your daily routines. Stop giving this killer any advantage. Don't worry about this too much. Together we will get to the bottom of this."

The officers left without finishing their tea.

Chapter

11

Mid-afternoon

Suzanne remembered something, just as
Corporal Bridges was placing her right index
finger into the ink pad. He was giving her
instructions, but she was barely listening. *Dariya
volunteers at the public library. Maybe she knows
something about the book. Or perhaps, she's the
anonymous tipster.*

"Can I have your left hand now, please?"
Bridges asked.

"Yes, of course."

An hour later, the Rickson's returned home
and immediately phoned a local locksmith. He
would come first thing Thursday morning. They
would have preferred tomorrow, but two days
wasn't unreasonable.

"I should take Nero for his walk," Charles said. "Would you like to come again? It was nice last time."

"I want to pay a visit to Dariya and Walter. Can you walk me there?"

"Why do you need to see them?"

"I have a couple of quick questions," she answered. "I know it's not your regular route. It's not a big deal. I can get there on my own."

"Nero and I don't mind a bit. Sometimes we need to deviate from our routines, isn't that what Laval advised us to do."

✶✶✶✶

Suzanne waited for her husband to wander away before ringing on the Underhill's doorbell. Walter answered the door, looked down at her, and hollered back, "It's for you, honey." He didn't even say hello to Suzanne. His breath reeked of whiskey, and his gray hair was a mess. Suzanne paid no regard to Walter's rudeness; she expected nothing less from the old curmudgeon.

Dariya emerged, looking a little tipsy herself. She was wearing a shabby nightgown that should have been discarded years ago. Their home stank of cigarettes. Suzanne had once smoked too, but she quit in her forties. Regardless of her earlier addiction to the deadly habit, she now held great disdain for anyone who still smoked. She placed those sentiments aside, grinned and said hello to her friend.

Walter turned and left. No doubt back to some mindless television show and a half-empty glass of cheap rye.

"What a pleasant surprise," Dariya said.

"Yes, well I was walking the dog with Charles, and while I was passing your home, I just wanted to remind you of the Mahjong game tomorrow."

"Oh, I wouldn't miss it for the world."

"Also," Suzanne hesitated, wanting to sound completely convincing. "I need to apologize. You see, I made you some jam but the police have confiscated it."

"Oh, that's alright, don't worry about it," Dariya said.

"Still, you probably heard that I gave some to Lan and Connie, and I didn't want you to think that I had neglected you."

"Oh, I know that," Dariya said. "I appreciate you telling me though."

"Certainly, we're old friends, right."

"Right, of course."

Suzanne turned to leave before employing a technique she'd learnt from watching Columbo. She pivoted back to Dariya and asked, "Do you still work at the Sechelt Library?"

"I'm a retired librarian. But I still volunteer three days a week. You see, I missed it so much. Why do you ask?"

Suzanne ignored her question. "If someone wanted to get a book out in someone else's name, could they?"

"Not without their library card."

"Could you personally do it? I mean could you loan out a book to a customer without their card?"

"Yes, of course, a librarian could, but the client would need to produce a valid picture ID. In general, clients should have their cards"

Suzanne took a short breath before asking, "Do you have access to all the patrons' accounts."

"Yes, of course."

"So you would know if... Charles or I took out a book."

"Say, what are you getting at?"

"Nothing. I'm just curious."

"Curious of what?"

"I was just wondering about the library's procedures and policies," Suzanne said.

"It's been my experience, that when someone wants to know all the details about our procedures, it's because they are up to no good." Dariya sounded flustered. "I know about the library book that the police found in your home."

How? "It was all just a misunderstanding; the police believe it was planted there," Suzanne said.

"And you think I did it!"

This wasn't how this conversation was supposed to go. "Heavens, no."

"I assure you I had nothing to do with this unruly behaviour. And I don't like your accusation that I could have anything to do with it."

"I'm not accusing you of anything. I would never…"

"Why hello, neighbours." Regina appeared from behind Suzanne.

Oh God, how long has Regina been standing there? What if she's been here for a while, eavesdropping on the two of us? There's no point asking her; she'd never tell the truth.

"Greetings, Regina. What a grand coincidence. Two surprise visitors in one day," Dariya said.

"Hello Regina, we were just discussing the Sechelt Library," Suzanne said, with every ounce of civility that she could muster. "Do you go there at all?"

"Good God no," Regina responded as if gravely insulted. "My son bought me a Kobo last Christmas. I love the little thing. Still, sadly I rarely have time to indulge myself in fiction. Besides, any half-decent novel is always made into a movie."

It was clear that Regina's snide comment was very much intended to be a thinly veiled insult. Dariya seemed unaffected by it, and Suzanne concealed her ire and said, "There are some excellent BC authors whom I'd be happy to recommend."

"Oh," Dariya added. "I bet you'd love Hawthorne."

"If I ever take a break from running this whole place, I'm sure I'll spend my time reading a dusty old book," Regina shrugged and smirked before turning to Suzanne, "I hope you liked the flowers," she said.

"Yes of course," Suzanne admitted. "They're beautiful. It was very kind of you."

"It was nothing. Adeline was a dear friend too. I will very much miss working with her." Regina said.

"I still can't believe that she's gone," Dariya said.

Regina held Suzanne's glare. "Life goes on, right girls."

Suzanne stared back at her rival, not wanting to be the first to blink. "Indeed."

"Well, I should be off, I'm sorry to have interrupted. I just wanted to say hello to my two dear friends," Regina waved her hand farewell and was off before the others could react.

****

What gall she had to refer to me as her friend, Suzanne thought on her way back. She got home just before the rain started up again. She could hear Charles playing with Nero upstairs. "I'm back," she hollered up.

"Great," Charles responded in return. He seemed to be enjoying his playtime as much as Nero was.

Suzanne stared at the vase containing the bouquet from Regina. She considered throwing them in the garbage again, but what would be the point? Save the dramatics and leave symbolism to the poets. She had a logical mind. She was capable of loathing the Ice Queen and yet accepting her gifts. She could appreciate beautiful flowers for what they were, beautiful. She leaned over and smelt the roses. Her ire gradually receded. Still she felt the urge to talk to someone, to have a conversation that had nothing to do with murder or Regina Snow. She picked up the phone and called Lisa. Her oldest daughter was always so self-absorbed in her own life, and she barely had time for the trivial matters of other people, even her own mother.

And that was precisely what the doctor ordered.

It was as if Lisa was standing by the phone, just waiting for someone to call her. "Oh mom, you won't believe what happened! We spent last night in Emergency," she said.

"What happened?" Suzanne asked.

"Don't worry. Nothing too major. Isaac got six stitches in the forehead. He went for a slide tackle at soccer and got kicked in the head, just over his eye. Blood was squirting out of his forehead like a firehose, but it looked far worse than it actually was."

"How's his eye?"

"It's fine. The cleat missed it by an inch, but it was a close call."

"Thank goodness... so he's fine."

"Yeah, he'll be alright. He might have a scar, but what boy doesn't have a scar on his head. Boys will be boys, right."

Raising two daughters had led to a couple of trips to the emergency room, but nothing was ever that serious. Come to think of it, both times were for Caroline. She twisted her ankle while playing tag once and sprained her hamstring in a high school track meet. Suzanne had been spared from the gushers on the forehead and other facial injuries. She never really understood the saying 'boys will be boys'. It was as if it excused reckless behaviour. She recalled when Lisa was in elementary school, the boys were playing in the forest, and one lad swung a large stick at another and smashed out two of his teeth. The next day at school, she had run into his mother, and she said the very same thing, "Oh well, boys will be boys." More and more Suzanne found herself thanking God for giving her two daughters.

Suzanne thought about debating the casual dismissal of young boys' violence towards each other. But she hadn't phoned Lisa for a dispute. "Sure, I guess," she said.

"Well, that was just the start of it. Isaac was howling as if he'd been shot. The blood scared him. We covered it up and took him to Lions Gate Hospital. I had to wait three hours to get his head stitched up."

"Did you have both boys with you?"

"No, luckily Mark was able to leave work early and stayed home with Tommy."

"Wait, when did you say this all happened?"

"Yesterday, around 7:30."

"7:30?" Suzanne repeated, "Mark left work early at 7:30! That's what you consider early?"

"Mom, drop it. You know he's on a big case."

"I know he's busy dear, but if 7:30 is early, when does he normally come home?"

"9ish," Lisa said sheepishly.

"Isaac and Thomas need to spend time with their dad."

"They see him. Don't be overly dramatic. It's just that Mark is busy right now," Lisa said.

"He's always busy. There's never a time that Mark is not busy. No wait, I take that back. If Mark isn't busy, he's golfing."

"Mom, Mark is a good father and provider." Lisa's voice was getting louder.

"Being a good provider isn't the same thing as being a good father. You may not have had as much growing up, but your father was always there for you. Kids can live without all their tablets and video games, but they need their dad." For the second time today, her conversation wasn't going as planned. Calling Lisa was supposed to be a quiet distraction. Suzanne needed to calm down.

"You know, life costs money. Flying the entire family home to see Grandpa costs money. Money that Mark provides for all of us. Isaac and Thomas are good kids. Plenty of children grow up without their dad watching over their every move. I'm here! I'm their mom, and I look after them. We all do our part. Mark does his, and I do mine."

"I'm not saying you don't do your part. You're an excellent mom," she said. Well most of the time she is, Suzanne thought. There was no point bringing up the whole vaccination incident; Lisa was already seething.

It was time for her to exit this conversation before it spiralled out of control. Lisa was clearly in one of her moods. It was never wise to engage her when she was like this. Suzanne made all sorts of excuses, like having to make dinner and having cookies in the oven. Little lies, she told herself. Just enough to get her off the phone. Suzanne had called Lisa to relax; instead she got herself even more riled up. Well, she sighed, at least I'm not thinking about Regina anymore.

Chapter

12

Wednesday, December 9th, morning

"**S**omething is wrong with the toaster," Charles said while making breakfast.

Suzanne had noticed it too. The bread hadn't popped up with its usual gusto. "It's fine, dear. Sit down and eat."

After breakfast, Suzanne got dressed and brushed her teeth. She returned to the kitchen to do the dishes, just as she did every morning while Charles was walking their dog. Surprisingly they were still home. Nero was turning in circles by the front door, and Charles was seated at the table, tinkering with the old appliance. "Careful, that thing is older than our children," she warned.

"It just needs a new spring," he said, and she smiled back. "Shouldn't take long."

She turned on the hot water and thought to herself, no one could ever accuse Charles of procrastination.

By the time the dishes were finished, the toaster's innards were sprawled across the kitchen table. What a surprise, she thought, the task is proving harder than his initial assessment. "It just needs a new spring, right dear."

"Don't worry, I know what I'm doing," Charles said without looking up.

"We need to go to Rona," she said.

"It's like you can read my mind sometimes," he smiled.

"It's not that hard, my love. Now go walk Nero before he has an accident."

****

While Charles was busy looking for the parts that he needed, Suzanne was talking to the employees, asking if anyone had seen Murray in the last few days. She spoke to some of his co-workers before tracking down the manager. So far, no one had seen him.

"It's not unlike him to miss a few days. He occasionally hits the bottle and disappears for a while," a handsome, blond clerk boy said.

"The police were here the other day too," a cashier revealed.

Suzanne thought that the store manager, Johan, seemed too young for his position. His face was peppered with acne, and his beard looked more like peach-fuzz. Still, he spoke of Murray warmly and seemed concerned for his well-being. "He's the best locksmith I've ever had," Johan said. "He has a true talent for it."

"Wait, Murray is a locksmith?" Suzanne asked.

"Well… not technically. He's been on a few company courses, but nothing official. He's a natural expert, I can tell you that. Most days he doesn't have to do much more than cut a few keys, but every once in a while, he'll fix a dozy of a jam. It's not a bad job for him; he doesn't have to stand lots or talk to many clients." Johan looked down at his watch. He seemed distracted.

"Was he bad at customer service?"

"You say you know Murray personally, right?"

"Yes, I've known him for years."

"Then you know that he has a quick temper when it comes to his speech impediment."

"I know him to be an emotional man, with a kind heart," Suzanne countered. She'd been told that it was the accident that changed him. He suffered a good blow to the head, and after that he was never quite the same. Murray worked hard at trying to appear normal. He had the heart of a child. He found joy in mundane occurrences, and he stuttered, especially when he was anxious. This unnerved many people, and they often jumped to conclusions that he wasn't an ordinary man. They were wrong, he may have been a tad simple, but he was far from being unintelligent. People's impatience and lack of tolerance occasionally enraged him, but much like the stuttering, he tried his best to keep it under control.

As the Ricksons drove home, Charles seemed eager to get back to his little chore. He had everything he needed to fix their beloved toaster.

Suzanne sat silently, contemplating her more significant dilemma. An important clue had just emerged that she wished wasn't true. Someone had entered their and Adeline's home undetected. The killer didn't force his way into their homes, because any evidence of it would have ruined their plot to frame her. So they would've needed a key or been able to pick the lock on the doors. Connie had the only spare key to her home. And as far as she knew, Lan was the only person to have had an extra key to Adeline's. Murray's locksmithing skills just put him higher up on her suspect list.

Upon arriving home, Suzanne phoned Caroline while Charles got back to work on the toaster.

After a few pleasantries, Suzanne asked, "You've seen the police reports, right dear? Do you know if there was any sign of forcible entry into Adeline's home?"

Caroline paused before answering, "No, the police found nothing."

"That's too bad," Suzanne said. "I was hoping that I was wrong."

"Why so?" Caroline asked.

"Never mind, it's not important."

"Hey, you don't get to 'never mind' me, you said this was our case."

Suzanne didn't like her daughter's tone, but she let it go. Caroline was under a lot of stress, she reminded herself. "Why the sudden interest?" she asked.

"I'm bored, I guess."

"How's the inquiry going?"

"Slow."

Suzanne needed her daughter's help, but she hadn't intended on involving her too much. Caroline was very much like her. They both liked to solve complex puzzles and became obsessed with it until completion. As a member of the Vancouver Police Department, Caroline had solved several high profile cases, but her means were often unconventional.

Her most recent case had been front-page news for weeks. The Independent Investigations Office was reviewing the incident to determine if Constable Rickson had used excessive force during her altercation with an alleged rapist. The inquiry would take several months, and Caroline was suspended with pay until it was complete.

Caroline was the type of person who didn't know what to do with her free time. Even as a child, she would set goals for herself and then become fixated upon them. For the past several years she had been immersed in her career within the VPD. Her suspension was perhaps only a road bump, but it was also giving her time to reflect. She had mentioned to her mother her fear of being a CFL. A constable for life.

"Here's a question for you, Mom. Who went to church with you on Sunday?"

"It was always the six of us. Charles and I, of course, Adeline, Dariya, Connie and Ivan," Suzanne answered.

"Great, we can take the five of you off the suspect list," Caroline said. Her enthusiastic tone conveyed that she was now completely emerged. "Now Regina says she was with Byron, and Anthony was at home with his wife. That leaves Murray and Lan."

"Surely you don't think that Lan did it?" Suzanne asked.

"I don't think anything yet, but Lan was alone and had access to Adeline's townhome."

Suzanne decided that Caroline's interest in this mystery would be a good thing. Perhaps it could be a distraction from her own life for a little while. She took some time and reviewed with her daughter that entirety of what she knew thus far. She reviewed some theories and didn't hold back her suspicions. Caroline listened intently.

After she was done, Caroline said, "So you think it was Regina who did it. You figure that while tending to Byron, she snuck out and poisoned Adeline."

"Well, I'm not so sure she had to sneak out of her own home."

"Ah, I see. You think that Byron is in cahoots with her."

Suzanne was pleased that her daughter was catching on quickly. "I'm not sure, but it's a possibility," she said.

"Okay, it's plausible," Caroline said. "But I have one question for you, how did they gain access to Adeline's home?"

"I'm not sure, but I can tell you that she's resourceful. If anyone could pull this off, it would be her."

Caroline didn't offer a counterpoint. "Oh Mom, I've also been doing a little digging on my own. Not about Regina, but rather in regards to your Staff Sergeant Laval. Don't be so trusting of him."

"He's alright." Suzanne wouldn't go as far as saying that she trusted him. She considered him a bright police officer, who was just doing his job. "He's very well-mannered and seems rather clever."

"Clever, yes," Caroline admitted. "But the overly-pleasant disposition is just part of his act. He's a good cop and bad cop rolled into one."

"How so?" Suzanne asked, thinking that her daughter was wedged in a cliché.

"He's known for his ability to form a good relationship with the accused. He'll act like he's your best buddy and that he's working for your interests. But all along, he's gaining intel on you. Just when you think that you've gained his trust, and perhaps revealed far more than you should have, he'll turn on you like a pit bull."

"Caroline Dear, you've always had a flair for the dramatic."

"Mom, he's thirty-four years old and a staff sergeant. He's the youngest person in his rank in Canada. Rumour has it that he ratted out his partner in Winnipeg. Mind you, his partner was dirty. Still, cops don't snitch each other out."

"I know the code, dear. Did you know that criminals have the same one?" Suzanne said.

"Nothing was ever made official, but his partner got an early retirement and Laval got transferred up to Yellowknife. It was made to look like a demotion, but instead, Laval quickly started jumping rank after rank after that."

"They don't just give anyone a promotion. I'm sure he earned his."

"He didn't earn it by being the nice guy," Caroline disputed. "He closes his cases, which the brass always likes. He has this line he likes to use, 'Together we'll get to the bottom of this.' He wants you to feel as though you and he are a team. But you're not, Mom. He's out to get you."

Suzanne cringed. He had said those exact words to her earlier, right before asking her to agree to be fingerprinted. Still, she didn't want to admit it to her daughter. "You're being absurd. I'm fully aware that we're not some sort of team. He didn't offer me any deputy's badge or anoint me his sworn alley. He's smart enough to know that I'm being framed, and that's smart enough for me."

"I know you think that you can confide in him and that he may appear as though he believes everything you are telling him. But at the same time, he's calculating the possibility that you are guilty."

"Then I have nothing to worry about because I'm not guilty."

"No, but someone is working very hard to make it appear as if you are. How long do you think it will take before they convince an ambitious officer willing to do anything to close a case? What if more clues are uncovered and they continually point to you? Eventually they'll convince Staff Sergeant Laval that you may have done it."

Suzanne was getting annoyed. Caroline shouldn't be questioning her. It's not as if she was fully co-operating with Laval. She hadn't even phoned him to report that Murray was a locksmith. She'd been feeling a tad guilty about it. Either way, both of her daughters were irritating her now. I guess it's too late to put them up for adoption, she thought.

They said their goodbyes shortly after. Suzanne's head was reeling with information. She found Charles in the kitchen, just as he was putting the casing back onto the toaster. "Success!" he cheered.

"I wish life were as easy as fixing a toaster," she lamented.

"It is honey," Charles said. "But not everyone can fix a toaster."

"Okay then. Sometimes I wish I was more like you, able to fix all of our little problems."

Charles walked over and wrapped his arms around her. "But then, who'd solve our big ones."

****

It was five minutes past four. The ladies were shuffling the Mahjong tiles, and Suzanne proposed that Dariya be the first dealer in honour of her first day as a regular.

"Oh, I can't tell you how happy I am to be able to play regularly," Dariya said. Despite her jovial tone, Suzanne sensed that she was a tad flustered. Maybe she was still irritated from yesterday's conversation.

"It's a pleasure to have you here, Dariya," Suzanne said while eyeing her suspiciously. It was unlikely that Dariya was the sole mastermind behind this entire plot. She could have easily taken the book from the library and contacted the police. But she's far too daft to have come up with the plan herself. No, she would've needed a partner. But that's not likely either, for who would be foolish enough to conspire with a known blabber-mouth.

"This still feels a little eerie to me, playing in Adeline's home like this," Lan admitted. She looked tired, and her hair was tied back. She hid behind a layer of make-up.

"It's like she's still here with us, dear. And that's a good thing." Connie said.

"Adeline would like this," Suzanne said. "She may even be watching us right now. She'd appreciate that we continued the tradition of using the guise of a friendly game of Mahjong as a means to natter."

"Oh, if we're just here to gossip, I don't know if I'll fit in," Dariya joked.

Everyone laughed.

"You'll fit in just fine, Dariya dear. We're an unruly bunch." Connie scoffed.

"Speak for yourself." Lan avoided eye contact.

"I'd rather be happy than dignified," Dariya said proudly.

"Charlotte Bronte." Suzanne smiled as she recognized the quote. Dariya often recited from her favourite novel, *Jane Eyre*.

"I think I'd rather be dignified," Lan said.

"That's because you've never been happy, and you don't know what you're missing," blurted out Connie.

Lan's face froze. Connie tended to let slip the most inappropriate comments. If anyone ever wanted to remain friends with her, they had to expect such unsolicited candour from time to time. This was perhaps the worst of times. It must have taken Lan's last ounce of sanity for her to pronounce, "You're probably right."

Suzanne concealed her shock. She needed to change the subject quickly, "So I'm sure you've all heard that the RCMP found a library book about poison in my home yesterday."

"Yes. And no one here believes it," Connie said.

"Well it's true," Suzanne said. "But someone put it there. I didn't steal a book from the library so that I could research poisons."

"Don't worry, dear. We all know that you're already fully versed in the deadly art of toxins." Connie was doing it again.

Suzanne ignored the comment and glanced at Lan. She seemed fine. Crisis averted.

Dariya looked into Suzanne's eyes and said, "And to clear the air. I didn't take the book and plant it in your home. Nor did I spread the rumour of the police's search of your home."

"And I believe you," Suzanne said.

It was Lan's turn to play, but she didn't budge.

Everyone waited in silence until Connie said, "Are you still playing, sweetie. We ain't getting any younger over here."

For a second, everything remained calm. Lan sat stoically as if there was no one else around her. Until she got up and said, "I can't do this. This isn't right." She rose from her chair and walked upstairs without another word.

And just like that, Dariya's first Mahjong game as a regular was over before it really began. But that was alright with Suzanne, for she had said everything that she had wanted to say and she heard everything that she needed to hear.

Chapter
13

Thursday, December 10th, morning

Suzanne was brushing her hair when she heard the doorbell ring. Nine o'clock on the dot. It better not be Laval making another unannounced visit, with more incriminating evidence against her. "Can you get it?" she hollered out to Charles. Moments later, she heard the door open.

"You should come down," Charles shouted from downstairs.

"Who is it? I'm not dressed."

"It's Lanny. You best bring a towel?"

Suzanne rushed down, unsure of what to expect. Was it an emergency?

Lan stood silently at in the doorway. A blank stare was painted on her face, and she was soaked to the bone. It looked as if she'd been there for a while.

Outside the winds were howling and the sky was dark. The rain was coming down sideways and slapped against the windows like ocean waves. It was a typical storm for this time of year. Inside, the home was cozy. Tea was steeping in the kitchen and the electric fireplace was cranked in the den. A benefit of a smaller abode is that it's easy to heat up. The bouquet from the Snows was in a vase on the kitchen table, and timeworn Christmas decorations were still displayed throughout the living area.

"Why haven't you invited Lan inside?" Suzanne said.

"I did."

"Come in from the cold, dear. You're letting all the heat escape," Suzanne said.

After what seemed like an eternity, Lan finally stepped inside, and Charles closed the door behind her. Lan's body couldn't stop shivering.

Suzanne was mortified to see her friend in such a state. She looked as if she'd been up all night. Heavy, black rings encircled Lan's bloodshot eyes. Her hair was frayed and matted, clumsily tied in a knot behind her head. She stood motionless in the kitchen, silent, wet, and defeated.

"Here, take this dear." Suzanne offered Lan the towel. "Let me get you a robe." She looked over at Charles, wordlessly dispatching him to fetch some dry clothes.

"I found a key," Lan said. She raised her hand to reveal a copper key with a label on its head, 'MW'. "Do you know where Murray lives? Would you like to check it out?"

An hour later, the Ricksons were out on the road. They had dried Lan off, fed her hot tea and convinced her to go home. Suzanne escorted her, dressed her in a comfy nighty and tucked her into her bed. Lan was asleep in minutes.

"Are you sure you know how to get there?" Suzanne asked upon returning to the car.

"I've only been there a few times," Charles answered. "It's kind of sketchy up there. It's all old logging roads. But yes, I think I can get us there. We have to go."

Regardless of Charles' words, Suzanne didn't like the idea of trekking up in the wilderness during a storm. Murray lived up there for a reason. So that no one could find him. She had called Connie and told her where they were going. "Just in case you need to call Search and Rescue to find us," she said. It was against her better judgment, but like Charles had said, they had to go.

The Ricksons drove into Sechelt and then passed through the Salish reserves. They travelled along old logging roads that Suzanne couldn't locate on her map. "Are you sure you're going the right way?" she asked for the umpteenth time.

"Yes," he said. But she sensed that he was unsure.

They stopped at an unmarked intersection. Charles looked up and down each way before turning right. "Are you sure..." she began to ask.

"I'm sure we're lost," he cut her off, and he smiled. "We're close. It's somewhere just over the next hill."

He continued driving north. He was concentrating as he maneuvered along a windy lane covered in puddles the size of swimming pools. The downpour was complicating the matter even further. Suzanne could sense his rising blood pressure. "It's alright if you can't find it, dear. I can't make heads or tails of where we are."

"No, this time I know we're close," Charles responded, his eyes never leaving the road.

"Alright."

"Biscuits," he cursed a few moments later. Charles halted fast and backed-up ten feet. He turned into an eroded driveway, acting as though he had planned the maneuver.

Suzanne didn't care. On any other occasion, she would have taken the liberty of noting that he was driving too fast, but today she was absolutely content to reach their destination in one piece. The trip had been harrowing for her.

It had taken every drop of her internal strength to remain calm.

The home that stood before them was smaller than Suzanne had envisioned. The craftsmanship was clearly Murray's. Great care had once been taken in the construction of this log cabin. But the years had not been kind to it. Clearly, minimal effort was made in its upkeep. The old-growth logs were starting to rot, and many of the windows had been boarded up. An antiquated satellite dish protruded from the roof, and an idle generator lay beside the west wall. Beside it sat a large rain bucket. The cabin was completely self-sufficient and off the grid. Murray's SUV was parked in front. Its tires were sinking into the earth, and the rain was slowly washing away the caked-on grime and tree sap.

"Maybe he's home," Suzanne said.

Charles examined Murray's vehicle. Its windshield was just as dirty as the rest of the body. "Nobody's driven that car for at least a week," he said.

The porch creaked as they stepped upon it. Charles knocked on the door, just in case its occupant had returned, but there was no response. The key turned effortlessly, and the door squeaked as they opened it. The Ricksons were instantly hit by a foul odour. It reeked of marijuana, stale booze and mildew.

"Hello. Murray, are you here?" Suzanne bellowed.

Still no answer.

Pizza boxes and empty bottles of Canadian rye littered the floor and tables. Mold was growing on dirty dishes in the sink. The two of them separated to find any clue to Murray's disappearance. Suzanne didn't want to go into his bedroom. Lord knows what she'd discover in there. She stayed in the main room and searched through the kitchen.

Several minutes later, Charles re-emerged and said, "Nada. Nothing but old clothes and dirty magazines. No sign of him being here in quite some time."

"I found something," Suzanne revealed. "Come here, but be careful not to touch anything."

Two empty tumblers stood on the kitty corners of a notification from the insurance company. It was clearly the policy that Adeline had taken out for Murray's benefit. On the bottom was scribbled: She always loved me. We should be together.

"Do you think it's a suicide note?" Charles contemplated out loud.

"Sure looks like it could be."

Just then they heard another car pull in behind theirs. They peered out one of the only unobstructed windows to discover a blue BMW.

A man got out and used a newspaper to shield his head from the rain.

Suzanne squinted in hopes of recognizing the visitor. "Do you know him?" she asked.

"I think it's Tony. That's his car."

"What's he doing here? I'm calling Staff Sergeant Laval. He needs to see this place anyways." For the first time ever, Suzanne wished that she had a cell phone. She remembered seeing a landline telephone under some old newspapers. She prayed to God that it still worked. God listened; there was a dial tone.

"Don't be paranoid," Charles said, but it was in vain.

Suzanne had already dialled Laval's number. She had it memorized. "Stall him," she ordered.

There was a knock on the door, and Charles ignored it. After the second knock Charles yelled, "Who is it?"

They heard Anthony yelling, but couldn't discern what he was saying. The rain hitting the roof had drowned out his hollering. Suzanne hung up the phone and signalled to Charles that is was okay.

Her husband opened the door and greeted Anthony.

"Lanny said that I'd find you here." Anthony smiled.

"Why are you here?" Charles asked.

"She thought that I could help. Perhaps I'll spot something that you missed."

"I have to ask," Charles said. "How are you so chummy with Lan?"

"I'll answer that one," Suzanne interjected. "Anthony, I bet you five dollars that I know exactly how you really met Lan and don't say that it was through the dentist office that she worked at."

"I never bet, Ms. Rickson."

"You see, that's the second time you've said that to me. But I've been to Adeline's home many times over the years and saw all the photos of her and you travelling together, back when you were married. She may have cut you out of all those pictures, but it's pretty obvious that it was you she travelled with."

"Yes, we used to travel a lot. We couldn't have any kids but had plenty of money. Why does that matter?"

Suzanne grinned. "It's where you went that is interesting: Las Vegas, Macao, Atlantic City. Adeline was never much of a gambler, but you used to be. And that's the common thread between you and Lan, and the reason why you're so secretive about it. You're both members of Gamblers Anonymous."

"You are as wise as Adeline said you were, Mrs. Rickson."

"Please, as we agreed before, call me Suzanne. And thank you." She felt smug and proud of herself. She also experienced a touch of relief. Anthony Wong was most likely not a threat.

Suzanne needed to keep Anthony in the cabin, so that she could witness his interaction with Staff Sergeant Laval when he arrived. Even though she believed that Anthony was innocent, she felt as though he was still withholding information. She estimated that the police would come in little over thirty minutes. She assumed the role of a gracious host as a means to stall him. "I've known Murray for a long time," she said. "And I know that he loves his coffee. I spotted a very out-of-place cappuccino machine in his kitchen. I can make us some coffees, but they'll have to be black. I wouldn't trust the milk we found in the fridge. Could I possibly make you something?"

Anthony looked puzzled. Perhaps he was not expecting such a warm invitation. Nonetheless, he accepted.

It took all three of them about five minutes to figure out how to make the contraption work, but eventually, they managed to get it to spit out three cups of smoking, hot coffee. They sat at the kitchen table, and Anthony spotted the insurance letter. He didn't say anything about it, and Suzanne wasn't about to bring it up. Instead they discussed Adeline, trading stories and keeping everything light.

Ten minutes later, a car pulled up into the driveway. They all went to the window, just in time to watch Staff Sergeant Laval step out of his vehicle. Anthony's facial expression revealed both surprise and apprehension, but only for fleeting second. He quickly regained his jovial visage.

Suzanne was also thrown off. He had arrived twenty minutes earlier than she expected. The drive here should have taken Laval much longer. Perhaps there's a shorter way up here that Charles is unaware of.

She offered to make more coffee, but Laval declined. He looked a touch sombre; his eyes were focused, taking in every detail. He was here on business.

"There, on the table," she directed Laval to the letter. "Don't worry, we didn't touch it," she added.

The detective put on a pair of latex gloves and lifted the letter. He read the letter twice while everyone remained silent. He took out an evidence bag from his coat pocket and placed the letter into it. "What are you all doing here?" Finally, he asked the question that he should have posed from the beginning.

"Lan sent us," Anthony said.

"I see." Laval nodded. His eyes rolled to the right. He was calculating something.

"I'm assuming you've been here and the RCMP have searched the residence," Suzanne said.

"I was here myself last Thursday."

"And the letter wasn't here," she said, more to herself than anyone else. "But since then, he left it in plain sight. From the looks of this place, I'd say he was on a bender ever since Adeline died. The pizza box has a receipt on it from last Saturday, the day before the funeral."

"Something else is bothering me." Suzanne looked up at Laval. "You seem preoccupied and you arrived here way too fast. Were you already on your way up when I called you?"

"Nothing gets past you, Ms. Rickson," Laval remarked. "Yes, I was almost here when you called. This letter helps to prove the suspicion that I had. You see, a corpse was discovered at Davis Bay this morning. The body was fairly bloated, which means it's been in the water for several days. It's too early to be certain of its identity, but I'm fairly sure that the deceased is Murray Wilthe."

Chapter

14

Mid-afternoon

Staff Sergeant Laval kept them at the cabin for over an hour. He had many questions. Other officers came and went, each with separate tasks. Suzanne was unaware that so many police officers were stationed in the Sunshine Coast; perhaps some had been brought in from the mainland to aid in the murder case.

Laval separated and questioned them individually. He was calm, to the point and polite. Still, Suzanne wondered if she was being considered as a suspect again. "Do you believe Murray's death to be suspicious?" she asked near the end of her interview.

"*Non*," Laval answered. "Not at this time, but we still need to investigate." Suzanne wasn't sure herself, and she didn't want to work it out with

154

Laval. She needed a quieter setting for such mental task.

At the beginning of the car ride home, she remained silent. She worked out the details in her head and constructed several theories. Charles didn't say a word as he drove. The rain had weakened into a light drizzle, and he no longer had to concentrate as much on the road. Murray's demise didn't seem to shake him up too much. He was doing what he always did, he was compartmentalizing his sadness. She knew that he'd grieve later, in private.

As they drove through the north end of Sechelt, alongside the Porpoise Bay Provincial Park and the native community, Suzanne wanted to talk things out and to see what Charles thought. "I'm sorry about Murray. I know he was a good friend of yours."

"Unfortunately, one of the drawbacks of growing old is outliving your friends and loved ones."

"Maybe, but it's still unfortunate."

"I hate to admit it," Charles said. "But I think Murray committed suicide. Nevertheless, I bet you suspect that he was murdered."

"Well, it sure looks like a suicide, but Adeline's murder was made to look like I did it. Someone is working very hard to conceal their crimes. So I think we have to consider the possibility that Murray was murdered."

"He was a troubled man," Charles said and paused. He must have assumed that Suzanne would interject. But she wanted to hear him out, so after a while, he continued, "The car accident and the loss of his first wife still weighed heavily upon him. He was always torn about his feelings for Adeline. He despised her for not marrying him and yet he always kept hoping that one day she'd change her mind because he loved her. Her death was one thing. But finding out that Adeline had been concerned about his well-being, by maintaining the life insurance policy, well, I guess, it was too much for him. That's pretty much what he wrote in his final note."

Suzanne considered before countering, "I'm just saying we have to look at all possibilities. Murray was a Catholic. He wasn't the type to take suicide lightly. He knew that he would be condemning his soul."

Charles remained silent. The notion of suicide was utterly foreign to them. Religion had long ago taught them that the ultimate sin was the taking of one's own life. The Ricksons had both lived blessed lives, and neither one of them had ever considered such a drastic option. Murray may not have attended mass often, but he was nonetheless very much a God-fearing man.

Suzanne got lost in her thoughts again as they drove into downtown Sechelt, and passed the

Rona store that Murray had worked at on Wharf Street. Charles appeared to be fighting back his tears. First Adeline, now Murray. "Darn it," he said, no longer concealing his frustration. "This isn't one of those books you read by Agatha Christie."

Suzanne took a breath. This wasn't a time to argue. She chose her words carefully and spoke calmly. "Well, someone murdered Adeline. There's no doubt in that fact. Isn't it conceivable that Murray knew something that could expose the killer? Maybe Murray was blackmailing him. Maybe it was always the killer's intention to murder them both. I admit, it looks very much like a suicide, but maybe that's what we are supposed to think."

"If that's the case, the killer would've had to plant the note and drown a grown man."

"The note would have been easy," she speculated. "Although not too many people would've been able to find Murray's home. He was quite the hermit and liked it that way. Only someone close to him could have done it. The drowning part might have been trickier but still feasible. Murray had been drinking for days. He may not have been too hard to subdue. An autopsy will reveal if he was breathing when he went into the water and if he was intoxicated."

They turned onto the highway and drove past the strip mall and police station. It seemed quiet for a Thursday afternoon. Traffic was rarely a problem in Sechelt, other than in a few moments in the summer when ferries brought in the tourists. They were almost home when Suzanne said, "How are we going to tell Lan?"

"I guess you want to speak to her alone again?"

"No, let's do it together." Suzanne disliked these kinds of situations, giving people bad news. Charles is far better at such matters. Besides, he'd always been very friendly with Murray, and it would be good for him to talk about it. Charles didn't object, and the conversation ended for a short while; she was contemplating on how to break the news to Lan.

It seemed like an unbearable task. Lan has been a wreck of late. The idea that Murray might have killed himself over Adeline's death might just be the final straw to her troubled emotional state. She was the last person to see him alive. What if she had said something to him? She already felt partly responsible for Adeline's demise. What if Lan blamed herself for Murray death too?

They chose not to go home, for Nero's sake. They were both tired and hungry, but if they popped in, had a snack and promptly left Nero alone again, it would be too much for him. So they drove past their home and parked four doors down, beside Lan's white Volvo. Telling her was something they had to do in person.

"What if she's still asleep?" Charles asked.

"We still need to tell her," Suzanne responded.

Lan answered her door almost immediately. "Oh, poor Murray," she sobbed.

Lan invited them in. Her unit was a tad smaller than their own, but it was filled with twice as much stuff. Tinfoil was spattered throughout her kitchen. The walls were greasy from too much cooking using a wok. Beneath the layers of oil were pink painted walls that were peeling in the corners.

Lan led them into her den. An unadorned Christmas tree, which was tucked into a corner, was the only decoration set up for the holidays. Lan slumped down in the middle of her faux-leather couch. Her sofa was overly big for the cozy living room and was the only place to sit. The Ricksons sat down on either side of her. Charles spoke first, "We were hoping you'd be still asleep. You need your rest." He sounded like a concerned father.

Lan explained that she couldn't sleep after they left her alone. So she had showered and got dressed. "I was determined not to live my life like a zombie and convinced myself that Adeline would want me to move on. Just then Anthony called, and I filled him in. He asked if it was alright for him to meet you guys up there."

"He asked if he could go to Murray's cabin?" Suzanne inquired. She recalled that Anthony had claimed that it was Lan who asked him to investigate. It was a minor detail, but still, one of them wasn't telling the truth and why lie about it?

Lan seemed a tad flustered with the question. She waved her hands, "I don't remember. Does it really matter?"

"No, please go on." No point getting her young friend even more unhinged.

Lan clenched her jade broach and continued, "I don't think Anthony ever liked him. Murray creeped him out. I guess he spooked a lot of people. But Murray was a gentleman. He always loved Adeline, and he was always nice to me. He lost so much in his life. He was one of the only people I ever felt comfortable talking to. I introduced him to Adeline, and she broke his heart. Everything is my fault. It's always my fault." Tears rolled down her cheeks.

Oh no, it's just as she'd predicted. Lan blames herself. Suzanne still needed to know something, but perhaps now wasn't the right times to pry. Could it wait? No, probably not. "How did you discover that Murray was dead?"

Lan regained a touch of composure and said very matter-of-factly, "Regina came by."

"How did she know?"

"I couldn't tell you. Regina always knows everything." Lan was sounding defensive.

"Was she alone?"

"Why so many questions? Have you been appointed a deputy or something?" Lan snapped. She didn't wait for an answer to her outburst before she just started to cry again.

Suzanne loathed hugging people, but she knew that she had to now. Lan was sobbing quietly, and it was precisely why Suzanne disliked such moments. Charles went into the other room to get some tissues and was taking far too long to return. She wrapped her arms around Lan and tried her best to be comforting. While holding Lan in her embrace, she couldn't help herself from scanning the room. She noticed that unlike Adeline's home, there wasn't a single photograph anywhere to be seen. Lan didn't want any reminders of her past.

"I should have stopped him on Saturday. I knew something was wrong," Lan said.

"Do you mean Thursday, dear?"

"What, yes, The last time I saw Murray was on Thursday. Has it been a week already? Oh, everything is a blur. Sunday was the funeral. Adeline's been gone for eleven days. And now Murray's gone too."

"Did you see Murray on Saturday or on Thursday?" Suzanne probed. Every little detail had to be accurate. "When did you see him last?"

"I don't remember anymore. Thursday, it had to have been Thursday. He always loved her, and he was going to prove it. That was Thursday."

"How was he going to prove it?"

Lan paused, she gathered herself. "I don't know. He didn't have to prove anything... everyone knew it. Adeline knew it, obviously. She..." she broke off into sobs, and Charles returned with the promised Kleenex. He sat down on the other side of Lan. Nothing was said for a while.

Soft music was playing from upstairs. Suzanne didn't recognize it, it sounded contemporary. The rain started up again and smacked against the windows. The wind whistled through the bare trees while the three of them sat on the couch.

After what felt like an eternity in purgatory, Charles broke the silence. "We should go look after Nero."

Suzanne took her cue to leave, "Oh my, the poor dog has been home alone for half the day." They got up to leave.

"Wait. Before you go, I have something for you," Lan said and hurried away. The Ricksons got their coats and shoes on as fast as they could.

Lan met them at the door and handed Suzanne a key. "It's to Adeline's place," she explained.

"Don't you still need it?" Suzanne asked.

"It's her key. I still have mine. Just in case something happens, you should have the spare."

Was Lan planning for something to happen? Either way, Suzanne liked the idea of having the key. It would allow her to snoop around and see if she could find a clue that Lan or the RCMP had missed.

They felt a little foolish driving only four townhouse-lengths home.

A note was taped to the door. Charles grabbed it and read it first. "Biscuits, we forgot about the locksmith. We booked him for this morning."

"I totally forgot." It wasn't like Suzanne to forget things, but Lan's early morning antics jarred the thought from her mind.

"The note asks if we could call him and re-book an appointment. That's awfully civil of him," Charles remarked and turned the key in the door. He fumbled with it a few times, before he said, "I think it's already open."

"How could you have forgotten to lock the door?" Suzanne accused.

"Honey, there's a murderer on the loose, I guarantee you that I locked the door."

Another odd detail occurred to Suzanne. Where's Nero? Why wasn't he there to greet them at the door as he always did? She heard him barking from behind their bathroom door. Suzanne scanned the room for any other disturbances and found another note. It was propped up on the table, leaning against the vase full of flowers.

Suzanne reached for the note as Charles said, "I'm going to let Nero out."

She put on her reading glasses and focused her vision.

> We are so fragile.
> You wouldn't think that
> Eating a plant,
> or going for a swim
> could be so fatal.
> We should all be more careful.
> Wouldn't you agree?

The seven lines were neatly typed on a cue card. Suzanne was speechless.

Nero appeared at her feet and licked her ankle. Charles was right behind him. "Well, what is it?" he asked.

Suzanne handed the card to him.

Charles read it aloud, and then a second time. "Maybe I shouldn't have touched this. There could've been fingerprints on it."

"No, the killer was smart enough to wipe the jam jar clean. She wouldn't have been sloppy with this," Suzanne deduced.

Nero ran in a few circles before making a b-line to his food bowl. "It's good to see that you are more hungry than traumatized. If only you could talk, boy. You could tell us who did this," Charles said.

Thank God Nero wasn't hurt. Her mind started asking questions. Is this a warning? Of course, it is. But why? Is the killer scared that I'm getting too close? How could he have done this? Anthony knew we were away. Who else knew? Is this proof that the killer was behind Murray's death too? No, it's not proof, but still a bold claim. But why mention it? Why would they implicate themselves in the two crimes? If the killer went to such lengths to frame her in Adeline's murder and to make Murray's death look like a suicide, why admit to it now?

And then something occurred to her. "Don't touch anything!" she screamed. "For heaven's sake, don't eat anything. I'm going to call Staff Sergeant Laval. Get outside!"

****

Staff Sergeant Laval and Corporal Bridges arrived thirty-five minutes later.

"Two phone calls in one day, you must like me, Ms. Rickson," Laval joked.

Suzanne frowned; she wasn't in the mood for his levity. "I wish that was the only reason I had to summon you again, Staff Sergeant," Suzanne explained the threatening letter and confinement of Nero.

"Somebody broke into your home in the middle of the day. That's very risky," Corporal Bridges said as he jotted down notes.

Laval looked at him in disapproval. Suzanne assumed that he had earlier been ordered not to ask questions. She wondered what the working relationship was between this older, more senior officer being out-ranked by a young hot-shot from out east. But it didn't really concern her now. She had more pressing problems to solve. She pondered the Corporal's statement, "Yes, I guess it would be a daring but, it's been stormy all today, so visibility isn't the best. And our neighbours that face us, the Kapoors, are away, visiting their family in India."

"So it's very likely that whoever broke into your home knew that you weren't in and that it was relatively safe to commit this crime in the day time," Laval concluded. "Did either of you two see anything out of place?"

"We didn't stay inside long enough to be sure," answered Charles.

"Do you mind if we come in and look for anything missing or suspicious?" Laval asked.

"Do you need a warrant?" Suzanne blurted out, sensing that Laval had ulterior motives.

"Not if you're inviting us in," Laval responded.

"Forgive my wife; she's feeling a little paranoid right now. Yes, of course, you can come in," Charles said.

"I'm sorry, yes," Suzanne said with a welcoming gesture. "Can I get you some tea?"

"No, thank you," Bridges entered the home.

"*Oui merci*," Laval answered.

"Oh, do you think it's safe to drink tea?" Suzanne proclaimed. Whoever broke in is most likely the person who poisoned Adeline. The killer could have tainted something in their home. Although, why would they leave the note? Still, it's best to err on the side of caution. Loose leaf tea would make an excellent method of injection. One could easily dry the leaves of a lily of the valley or foxglove and conceal it inside a tin of tea.

Laval caught on quickly, "Do you have anything pre-packed?" It was much harder to taint a teabag.

Suzanne sighed. Today was getting worse with every waking moment.

****

After the police left, Suzanne didn't know what to do. She called her best friends. Connie and Ivan were all too happy to invite the Ricksons over for dinner. The men insisted on washing the dishes. "You girls take a break," Ivan said. "Have some tea and sit down. Relax, that's an order."

Suzanne was all too happy to comply. They retreated into the living room. Connie, being a glass-half-empty person, kept repeating all the evil things an intruder could've done to them. "I wouldn't eat any of the food you have at home," she warned. "He could have poisoned anything and everything."

Suzanne was perturbed that Connie assumed that it was a man. "Poison is usually the method used by female killers, not men," she pointed out.

Connie must have known better than to engage her. Suzanne was in a foul mood and arguing semantics wouldn't improve her disposition. "Be strong, Suzanne. Just like I taught you."

Suzanne may have considered herself to be strong-willed, but even she had to admit that Connie was about as resilient as they come. She was reminded of this by a photograph in the living room of a much younger Connie chained to a cedar tree. A heavy-set lumberjack loomed over her. He looked as if he wanted to chop Connie down along with the tree.

Connie often retold the story behind the photo. It was taken in Clayoquot Sound during the summer of 1993. She was a member of Greenpeace and along with fellow environmentalist and First Nations bands peacefully protested against the forest industry and won. She always ended her tale by saying, "To this day, Clayoquot Sound is protected land."

"Thank you," Suzanne said to her closest friend. "I will be as tough as you."

The two women sat for a bit, drank their tea and eavesdropped on their husbands. The two men were having a lively debate about hockey. Suzanne stopped paying attention. Her thoughts drifted to the warning that Caroline had given her earlier. Maybe Connie could help. "Listen, I need to ask you a question," Suzanne said.

"Shoot."

"Did Staff Sargent Laval ever interview you?"

"Only once, shortly after Adeline passed," Connie answered.

"Did he ask you anything about me?"

Connie thought for a moment. "No, not directly."

That was a curious response. "What do you mean?"

"He asked about the rumour," Connie responded sheepishly. She rubbed the back of her hand, just like she did in Mahjong whenever she was anxious.

Suzanne cringed. "And what did you say?"

"That is was tripe."

"How can you be so sure?"

Connie's face tightened. She sat up and looked Suzanne in the eyes. "Because nothing gets by you, and Charles couldn't lie out of a speeding ticket. If he were ever unfaithful to you, you'd likely know about it before him." She laughed.

Their husbands walked into the room, carrying two beers. They seemed jovial and carefree. The women's conversation ceased instantly. "What were you two talking about," Ivan asked.

"Nothing," Suzanne answered. She had lots to think about. Laval had been looking into her possible motive to harm Adeline. Was he looking into her? Perhaps Caroline was right; she should be more wary of the charming detective. She desperately wanted to go home and relax. But was their home safe? She needed

to be alone, and her house was as secure as anywhere else. The killer had to be caught before Suzanne could ever feel truly safe again.

Chapter

15

Friday, December 11, morning

Charles phoned the locksmith as soon as it opened the next day. The notion that Murray could have done the job, if only he were still alive, crossed Suzanne's mind but she didn't mention it to Charles. He was probably thinking about it too, and neither of them wanted to say it.

Together they completed the task of emptying their fridge and pantry. Anything that wasn't securely sealed had to be tossed. Suzanne was furious to be throwing away so much good food. She tried to convince herself that if the killer had wanted her dead, there wouldn't have been a note. Still, there was no point taking any chances with their lives.

Suzanne phoned Caroline and explained what happened.

"It's not up for debate, Mom," Caroline said on the phone. "I'll be on the 1:20 ferry."

Suzanne often said that Caroline had been born from the same fabric as her father. She was naturally laid back and calm, but certain events in her life changed her forever. Now she was jaded. The notion that someone had threatened her parents could only lead to one reaction; she had to be there, to protect them. Who better for the task than an officer in the VPD? Suzanne was confident that no one would mess with them as long as she was staying under their roof. Or at the very least, she'd like to see them try.

In the past, Caroline had often cautioned her parents that their home wasn't adequately secured. Charles had always retorted, "This is the Sunshine Coast, kitten, not East Vancouver." Suzanne had agreed with him. Now she wished that they had listened to their daughter's advice.

Suzanne spent the morning taking inventory of her home. Thank God, none of her jewelry was missing. Nothing she owned was overly valuable, but each piece was precious to her. There was a brooch that her favourite aunt had given her on her sixteenth birthday and a ring that had been her great grandmother's. Her prize procession was a purple heart awarded to her father during the Second World War. He had been shot on the beaches of Normandy but stayed in the battle until it was won. It signified the legacy of her family's lineage; they saw things through to the end.

Charles went out for his morning walk with Nero. He was reluctant to leave Suzanne, but she shushed him away. She needed to be alone in her home to get over her dread that she'd never feel safe again. There was nothing to fear, but fear itself, she told herself. She put her father's medal into the pocket of her robe and set forth to make a cup of coffee.

She felt a pang of guilt for not phoning her father more often. She had hardly recognized him this autumn when she travelled home to Montreal. The frail, old man who spent his days lying in bed watching TV, was once as strong as a bull with broad shoulders and a permanent smile. As a child, she was mesmerized by the scar on his left shoulder. Just thinking of it gave her strength. She went into her living room and put Duke Ellington, *Live at Carnegie Hall* onto her record player. It was his favourite record.

Just as she sat down, the phone rang.

True to his word, Staff Sergeant Laval was calling to keep her informed. "I'm afraid I've nothing but bad news for you, Ms. Rickson," he said. "The coroner has positively identified the body from yesterday as Murray Wilthe's. My condolences, I realize that you and he were friends."

"Charles was closer to him. He was a very kind person. Did the coroner say anything else?"

Laval paused. Perhaps he was contemplating how much to reveal. Suzanne didn't push. Eventually, he said, "It's too early to do a thorough examination. The body has been transported to Vancouver. I can tell you that there was water in his lungs."

"Which means that he was alive when he went into the water," Suzanne said.

"It is consistent with a suicide by drowning."

"Or someone forced him underwater."

"Possibly."

Suzanne perceived insincerity in Laval's tone. It was pretty clear that he surmised that Murray had taken his own life, but Suzanne wasn't wholly convinced.

"On an interesting note," Laval said. "Did you know that Mr. Wilthe had a son?"

"No, he never mentioned one."

"To be more precise, he's Mr. Wilthe's stepson, from his first marriage to Lilith May. His name is Robert May, and he lives in Arizona. Father and son had been estranged for a very long time. I spoke to him yesterday. Mr. May didn't have a kind word to say about his departed stepfather. He has no intention of coming up to sort out his stepfather's estate."

"This is all news to me," Suzanne said. "Murray never mentioned a stepson. He always said that they had no children."

"Robert May isn't worth bragging about. He was, however, happy to discover that he was Murray's only living heir. We have been reviewing Mr. Wilthe's financial affairs, and he was quite wealthy, even before Adeline's life insurance policy."

"We knew that Murray had some money, but we didn't know how much. I mean, he still worked at Rona. It's funny, you've seen his cabin. He lived like a hermit," Suzanne said.

"Human behaviour will never stop surprising me, Ms. Rickson. For instance, the library book we found on your bookshelf on Tuesday, it was checked out by you three weeks ago."

"I did no such thing." Suzanne held the telephone tighter.

"I believe you, but your card was scanned at the library on November sixteenth. It was only used to check out one book, the first book you've borrowed in several years."

"As I said before, I stopped going to the library ever since we started swapping books at the seniors' centre."

"I remember you saying that. But did you still keep a library card?" Laval's voice remained calm, with no hint of accusation.

"Yes. I don't think I ever took it out of my wallet. Let me go find it." Suzanne laid down the phone and retrieved her purse. She rummaged through her wallet for several minutes before returning and declaring, "It's missing."

"Do you keep your purse with you at all times?" Laval asked.

Her head was reeling. How was this possible? What was going on? "No, I often leave it at home. Like for walking the dog … or going to church. This is so absurd. The killer didn't just steal the book from the library and plant it here."

"No, they thought up an even more incriminating scenario."

Here's what I suspect," Laval said. "The killer has been planning this for quite some time. November fifteenth is a Sunday. They must have known that you'd leave your purse at home and assumed that the card would be in it. They waited until you left for mass, entered your home and stole the card. On the next day, they used it to check out the book from the library. They may have tried to return the card when planting the note. But if I remember correctly, you had your purse with you at Murray's cabin."

"I did." She was impressed with Laval's observational skills; perhaps they even matched her own.

"Not being able to return the card wouldn't have been a major issue. It's a minor detail."

"That means the killer has been watching me for a very long time. They've been studying me." Suzanne sighed.

"Yes. The killer is detail-oriented and well organized. I've sent the letter and the library book to the lab in Vancouver for fingerprinting and analysis. I highly doubt we'll find anything."

Suzanne considered his theory to be viable. It means that the killer had broken into their home on numerous occasions. It was almost eleven o'clock, and the locksmith couldn't arrive fast enough. She wasn't going to leave her home, or even blink an eye until all the locks were changed.

****

Suzanne poured herself another cup of coffee. The whole affair was getting out of hand. As she peered outside her window, she saw a blue BMW emerge from out of the fog and drive past her home. What's he doing here? She noted the time, 11:15 AM. The locksmith should be there soon. She stood by her front window and waited for Charles and Nero to return from their walk. Finally they appeared. "Are you going anywhere in the next little while?" she asked.

"Nope."

She had no desire of leaving her cozy home and going out into the blustery cold, but she knew that she had to. Charles could remain and wait for the locksmith. She needed to talk to Anthony.

Outside was unseasonably chilly. The sun was just starting to burn away the morning mist and promised a bright and clear day. It was early December, and no snow had been forecasted. Suzanne didn't miss the harsh winters of her childhood one bit. She could deal with a little fog and rain, no problem.

She hoped that Anthony had stopped at Lan's house, but there were no cars in her driveway. Her next assumption was that he had gone to Adeline's. Where else would he go? Maybe Lan will be there too, and perhaps if she could sit them both down at the same time, she'd be able to get a straight answer out of them.

She arrived at Adeline's to find Anthony's car, but not Lan's. That's strange. Was it safe to confront Anthony alone? He seemed genuine. But what if he's not? Why was he here? To talk to Lan? But if she's here, where's her car?

The door was locked tight. Suzanne had left her key at home. She hesitated for a moment before ringing the doorbell. Anthony Wong opened the door with his trademark grin. "Suzanne, what a pleasure."

"Save it Anthony, what are you doing here?"

Anthony must have been taken aback from Suzanne's directness, but he hid it well, "I'm looking for Lan. I spoke to her yesterday, but I couldn't reach her today."

"You're worried about her? Why?" Suzanne was starting to worry too.

"I can't say." For the first time ever, Suzanne noticed lines around Anthony's eyes. He looked unnerved.

"You can't, or you won't say?"

"I can't."

"Considering the nature of your relationship, I can guess why you're concerned."

"Come in, Suzanne. You'll catch a cold outside." Suzanne was wearing an old winter coat which she'd brought from Montreal. She wasn't cold in the least, but she was curious. So she accepted Anthony's invitation.

Adeline's living room looked immaculate. Everything was in order, and there was no clutter. Fresh-cut, white roses were in a purple vase on the coffee table. It was as if Adeline's ghost was still living here and keeping everything in order.

"Did you bring those roses?" Suzanne asked, pointing to the vase.

"No," he said. "What would be the point?"

Exactly, Suzanne thought. Why bring white roses to a dead women's house? Lan must have done it, but why? White symbolized purity and innocence. Then she remembered that in

Chinese culture white is the colour of mourning.

"Anthony, I hope you don't mind me asking, but how did you get in here?" Suzanne softened her tone so as not to sound as though she was accusing him of anything.

Anthony flashed his smile. He reminded her of an Asian Robert Redford. That smile just came automatically. It was disarming. "I have a key," he said.

Really? Adeline guarded her privacy. It's not surprising that Lan had a key to her home, but her ex-husband had one too. Who else may have had easy access? In Suzanne's moment of contemplation, Anthony asked, "Didn't she give you a key too?"

Suzanne couldn't be sure if his comment meant to be an insult? Stay calm. She took a breath before answering, "No." It was all she cared to admit.

"Can I get you anything?" Anthony offered. It was as if he felt entirely at home.

"No, thank you." Suzanne eyed Anthony intently. She was looking for clues and found none. "So, are you worried that Lan is sitting at a roulette table in Reno?"

"No," Anthony said as he sat down onto Adeline's couch. He crossed his legs and stretched out his arms. His gray suit fit all too well. "Between you and me, she was always partial to slot machines."

"You don't approve."

"Statistically speaking, the money slots are a gambler's worst option. They are rigged for the house's biggest returns."

"You would have preferred baccarat perhaps, better odds." Suzanne felt the urge to flaunt her knowledge of gambling. She rarely spoke of the subject, but knew her fair share from reading the exploits of Sir Ian Flemings's James Bond.

"Back in my day, when I used to lose my shirt to the merciless gods of gambling, Baccarat wasn't readily available unless you were sitting in a casino in Monte Carlo. I myself was always fond of Blackjack. Fortunes could be made or taken away in a single hand. Sadly, in my case, they were mostly taken away."

Suzanne really didn't care to hear about Anthony's foolish gambling exploits. She was far more concerned about Lan. "Casinos are everywhere nowadays. Do you think that Lan is back on the dragon and sitting in a casino in Vancouver?"

Anthony laughed, "Not exactly. The dragon is a reference to heroin, not gambling. But I can say that a gambling addiction is in many ways similar to a drug addiction. An addict is never fully cured. It's in our blood to seek out that which makes us the most happy. Regardless of its effect on ourselves or our family. So yes, between you and me, I am very concerned that Lan is back in action. In fact, I'm pretty sure she is. She told me yesterday that ever since Adeline passed away, she'd been sneaking off to casinos again. When she didn't answer my calls this morning, I rushed over here right away."

Anthony was being very candid for a change. It was unlike him. So Suzanne decided to take a chance. "What do you know about the engagement ring that Murray gave to Adeline?"

"I think I know the ring." Anthony's tone was grave as if he was being accused of something and wanted to clear the air. "About four years ago, Adeline asked me for a loan. We were just starting to reconcile, and it was just like the Adeline of old, she was asking for money again. But this time she had collateral." Anthony paused as if to gather his thoughts and Suzanne showed interest by taking a seat on the armchair.

"Maybe it would best if I start from the beginning," he said. "I know how it looks. I left Adeline for a younger woman. But what she probably never told you was that Adeline and I were never really happy together. Sure, we travelled a lot, but I wanted a family, and she didn't..."

"She couldn't," Suzanne cut him off. Anthony looked confused, so she elaborated.

"Lan told me that Adeline couldn't have children."

"In all the years I've known Adeline, she always insisted that she just didn't want to have a family. She never told me that she couldn't. Even after her death, I'm still uncovering little secrets that she kept... Well, you can clearly see why we argued like crazy. One of us had to end it."

Anthony sighed before saying, "Falling in love with my secretary is rather cliché, but I assure you it wasn't intended. Either way, it happened. I may have been still living with Adeline, but we hadn't shared our bed for a long time. Regardless of my infidelity, our divorce was inevitable. Don't get me wrong. I have guilty feelings about how things went south between us. I will always love her." Anthony paused again, and Suzanne was getting the impression that this speech had been rehearsed.

"I was elated when after many years Lan stepped in and reunited us. But it didn't take long for Adeline to start acting like her old self. Within a month of our reunion, she asked to borrow forty thousand dollars. She refused to tell me why she wanted the money and insisted that I keep it a secret between us, especially to Lan. I was going to refuse. But as I mentioned earlier, she had collateral, a two carat yellow diamond ring. I had it appraised, and it was worth far more than the forty K that she was asking for. So

I gave her the money. We agreed that I'd pay her five-hundred dollars less for her monthly alimony and I would hold onto the ring until we were square again. She was over halfway to repaying me when she passed away."

"Truthfully, I wasn't sure what to do then. I was going to talk to Lan about it, but I knew that she wouldn't have the remaining money that Adeline owed me. Nor did I want to betray Adeline's wishes and reveal to Lan the arrangement that we had." Anthony looked up as if trying to gain Suzanne's empathy.

"A few days before the funeral, Murray showed up at my office. He offered me forty thousand to get the ring back. I don't know how he knew about it, so I presumed that Adeline had told him. I informed him that Adeline's debt was partially paid and that she only owed me seventeen thousand more. He went back into his car and returned with the exact amount in cash. I had always assumed that it was Murray's engagement ring to her. So I gave it back to him, it seemed like the right thing to do."

"Were you hoping to find the ring when I met you at Murray's house yesterday?" Suzanne asked.

Anthony sighed, "I'll admit it. The thought did cross my mind. Even more so when the police showed up and told us that he was dead. It's probably lost forever now. The police never mentioned finding it. So I assume that Murray had the ring with him when he jumped into the ocean."

Or when someone drowned him in the ocean, Suzanne thought.

"It's a real pity," Anthony said. "It was a beautiful ring, and worth a lot of money. Lan could have used it. Maybe it would have stopped her from spiralling out of control."

"Actually," Suzanne said. "Murray's son, Robert, would've inherited it. And from what I'm told, it's

probably better off in the ocean. At least it's more romantic."

"Murray had a son?"

Suzanne was watching Anthony intently, looking for reactions, much like Laval had observed her. "Robert is his son from his first marriage. He's the sole inheritor of Murray's estate. From what you're saying, the ring would rightfully be his."

"Romance be darned," Anthony said. "I hope Murray didn't do anything foolish. I hope we find that ring. I fully disavow any claim to it, and if I'm the one that finds it, I promise that I will give it to Murray's son."

"But you have no knowledge of where it is now?" Suzanne asked, the skepticism thick in her voice.

"I swear to you, I gave it to Murray and I haven't seen it since."

Suzanne wanted to believe him. "Do you figure that we should notify the police?" Once again softening her tone to keep Anthony at ease.

"Maybe."

That wasn't really an answer. Suzanne had the impression that no matter how hard she tried to manipulate Anthony, it was he that was using her.

Chapter

16

Lunchtime

The locksmith had come and gone while Suzanne was at Adeline's. Charles reported that he was quick and efficient. He had purchased the most expensive locks available. As long as they secured their rear screen door, no one could unlawfully enter the home, unless they broke a window. The locksmith assured them that short of an alarm system, this was the most protected they could be. Suzanne felt better already.

Suzanne sat down and took everything in. So much was happening so fast. She felt overwhelmed. She wanted to grieve for Murray, yet it just didn't seem to be the appropriate time for such an emotional release. She was full of sorrow, anger and contempt, and none of these emotions were helpful in her pursuits. She had to uncover Adeline's murderer, after that she could cry and scream if need to, but not before then.

Just after three o'clock, there was a loud knock on the door. Nero barked once, and Charles met his daughter at the front entrance. Standing at five foot eleven, Caroline was taller than both her parents. When she was a kid she drank a lot of milk and grew like a weed. Her brunette hair was tied back in a bun, and she wore little make-up, a trait she mimicked from her mother.

Caroline had always been slender. Even at thirty-six, she maintained her runner's body. She had long legs and powerful muscles. She had once dreamt of being an Olympic athlete, but an accident on the track ended her aspirations. Even though her dreams of being a top-rated athlete were quashed in high school, her passion for running never diminished.

Caroline was all smiles as she hugged Suzanne. She had packed very little but told them that she was willing to stay as long as she was needed. While Nero ecstatically ran in circles around her, Charles put the kettle on for tea.

Once Caroline was settled in, the Ricksons sat at the kitchen table for tea time, a British tradition they had long upheld. With a teacup in one hand and a cookie in the other, Suzanne relayed all that Staff Sergeant Laval had revealed earlier that morning. "He's a nice man. You'd like him, Caroline."

"Mom, stop."

"I'm just saying."

"Someone is trying to frame you for murder, and you're worried about not having more grandchildren." Caroline put down her cup tea. She hadn't touched her cookies but looked at them often.

"That's not true. We're not worried about that at all," Suzanne said.

"You've made it perfectly clear that you are not interested in starting a family and we respect that," Charles added for measure.

"Sure you do." Caroline rolled her eyes.

Suzanne knew very little of her daughter's love life. She knew that Caroline had been in a serious relationship when she was in the Army while serving in Somalia. It ended badly. When she returned home from duty, she quit the Army and promptly joined the VPD. She made a grand declaration that she was not interested in dating a police officer. Rumours spread when she befriended an openly gay forensic doctor, but Caroline always insisted that they were just friends. Suzanne often wondered if Caroline would ever come out to her if she were a lesbian.

Suzanne had often spoken about how she was worried about Caroline. She thought that her daughter worked too hard and that she'd grow old alone. Caroline had been married to her job for too long.

Charles had voiced different concerns. He had told Suzanne that with Caroline's career in jeopardy, she was probably really stressed. "Are you alright?" he asked warmly.

"I'm fine," Caroline said nonchalantly. "Let's stick to the case. You know that we're supposed to be going to Montreal in a week. Let's make sure that you don't get arrested before then."

"Don't be silly, dear," Suzanne said. "We're not going to be arrested. I've been assured that we are not suspects."

"By Laval?" Caroline asked. "He's crafty, and you shouldn't trust him."

"It's not a matter of my trust in him or my lack thereof. I find him to be intelligent and competent."

"Your mother has a crush on him," joked Charles.

"Stop it," Suzanne scowled, before changing her tone. "Although he is quite handsome." She winked.

"Arrrgh! You're doing it again," Caroline said. "Enough with the matchmaking."

"I was doing no such thing. I just find his accent refreshing, and he has alluring eyes." Her last statement was more of a jab at Charles than anything else.

"Are you done?" Caroline sounded annoyed. "Our best defence against whoever is trying to frame you is to solve this crime. Do you still think that Regina is behind it?"

Suzanne couldn't hold back. "Everything points to her. Her alibi is pretty weak."

"But not having an airtight alibi doesn't seem to match our killer's profile. He broke into your home two weeks prior to the murder. That takes a great deal of premeditation. If Regina was calculating such a plot, wouldn't she have found a better alibi than staying at home with her husband?" Caroline deduced.

"That's true," Charles said.

"And would she have the capability to break into Adeline's and your home undetected?" Caroline added.

"No, probably not," Charles agreed again, and Suzanne remained silent.

"Okay, who else do we have?" Caroline asked. "I know that you don't like the idea, but your friend Murray could have committed the murder. He's the scorned love interest, which is pretty much the strongest motive there is. He may have been overwhelmed with guilt once he discovered the life insurance policy and committed suicide."

Suzanne didn't like this theory, but she considered it before saying, "He couldn't have broken into our home to plant the threatening letter. He would've already been dead."

"Maybe he got help? A two-person job." Caroline said.

"No, Murray wasn't the type of guy someone would plan a murder with. He was too unpredictable."

"What if he got help from Lan?" Caroline suggested. "They both profited from Adeline's death, and you've said before that she and Murray go way back. Lan may be the only person in the world who would have trusted Murray. You've mentioned that she hasn't been herself of late. Maybe she's fraught with guilt too."

Suzanne sat quietly as she mulled over the possibility. Could Caroline be right? Could Murray and Lan have done it together?

Charles broke the silence, "Lan already had access to Adeline's suite. And what if Murray taught Lan how to pick a lock? With his knowledge, she could've broken into our home."

"Possibly," Caroline said. "Or have either of you ever gone to him to make a key at Rona? He could have made an extra copy then and given it to Lan."

"No," Suzanne said. "We just discovered that Murray was a locksmith."

"Murray was a locksmith?" Caroline said. "You didn't tell me that before. That changes things."

"No, it doesn't," Suzanne said. "It just means that he was capable of breaking into our home. But it doesn't prove anything." She shifted her weight in her chair and took a sip of tea. Reluctantly, she had to admit that Caroline's theory was plausible.

"I liked Murray, but he was always a little quirky," Charles admitted. "I've seen him lose his temper for the smallest of reasons. He tried to control it, but it got the better of him on occasion. But I still can't see him harming Adeline."

Caroline scratched her head. "Neither Lan or Murray ever came to church, but they knew that you and Adeline would be at mass on Sunday mornings. They could've used those opportunities to enter your homes, poison Adeline and frame you."

"Fine, I'll concede they had the means..." Suzanne said.

"And the financial motive," Charles cut her off.

Suzanne veiled her displeasure of being interrupted and stayed on course, "Okay, they had the means and the motive, but I doubt they are the type to murder someone, let alone a dear friend."

"People can surprise you," Caroline said. "As a cop, I see this kind of stuff all the time, and

I'm still stunned sometimes at how cruel we can be to each other."

"Okay. But to be frank, I doubt either of them had the brains and foresight to conjure up such a scheme. We're not talking about the sharpest of knives here..." Suzanne said.

"But let me guess," Charles said, "Regina could have?"

"Stop interrupting me."

"You were done your sentence," Charles protested. "Other people can talk too, you know."

"Will you two stop your bickering?" Caroline slammed her palm against the kitchen table.

"We're not bickering... and yes, back to my point. Regina Snow is very much capable of murdering someone for her own benefit, as long as she could get away with it. It's in her nature," Suzanne said. "Something else has been bothering me too."

Charles rolled his eyes but didn't say anything.

Suzanne ignored him and continued, "We all accepted that Regina didn't have a motive because she had manipulated the election and wasn't in risk of being usurped. She says that she has signed proxies that would have guaranteed her victory."

Caroline must have caught onto her mother's point for she said, "But has anyone actually seen these proxy votes?"

"She didn't need to produce them since no one is running against her now," Charles said.

Suzanne was pleased that they were all seeing her point. To add fuel to her argument, she continued, "And since we're debating the possibility of a partnership, what if she recruited someone else to help her?"

"It's possible," Caroline agreed. Her willpower must have finally snapped, she grabbed a cookie and ate half of it in the first bite.

"The more I think about it, the more I consider this to have been a two-person job. I bet even when Regina visited Lan to tell her that Murray was dead, what she was really doing was acting as a lookout while her accomplice broke into our home and planted the warning."

"Do you think that Byron helped her?" Charles wondered.

"Well sure. Byron ensured that everyone knew that he was feeling ill. It could have been all part of their plan. He usually keeps to himself."

"I guess," Charles agreed as he massaged the back of his neck.

"Just think about it. In the past, if Byron were sick, you just wouldn't see him for a few days and then a few days later he'd tell you about in passing. No big deal. This time he does this grand production. He was setting a plausible scenario in order to give Regina an alibi. We all had to know that he wasn't well. Just so that all of us would accept the possibility that Regina was home with him all Sunday. Even if she was, it doesn't mean that she couldn't have sneaked out for a little while."

"I'm not saying no," Caroline said. "But I still have two concerns. One: like I said before, if Regina and Byron were our killers, the masterminds behind breaking into your homes and planting incriminating evidence and devising all of this for at least two weeks in advance, they would have contrived better alibis than just each other. And two: would they have had the ability to access your homes?" She finished the cookie.

"Byron is a pretty bright fellow. He could've been practicing how to pick locks in his living room. If they've been planning this for a while, he'd have the time to figure it out," Charles said.

"It's not that easy, Dad. Even before you got that new deadbolt, the old lock you had wasn't that bad. It would have taken more than just an amateur to break into your home."

They all sat quietly for a while. As far as they knew, only Murray would have had the skills to pick their locks. "What about Regina's son?" Caroline pondered. "What do you know about him?"

"Not much, he's a fisherman by trade. We saw his pick-up parked in the last stall of the visitor parking for days before Adeline's murder. Regina and Byron deny it, but that's not surprising. I don't know if he would have been able to pick our locks," Charles said and drained his tea.

"Not so fast, didn't someone once tell us that he had served time. Wasn't it for breaking and entry?" Suzanne said.

"I don't remember... but now that you mention it. It does sound a little familiar." Charles turned to look at the kettle. Probably thinking about making more tea.

"We need to know for sure. Has Regina's son ever been arrested? Can you find out, dear?" Suzanne said, turning to her daughter.

"Not as easily as I could if I were working. Plus your Staff Sergeant Laval is a pretty bright man. I could get into some serious trouble if he ever found out that I was doing a criminal record check for personal reasons."

"I don't think so," Suzanne said. "He seems to be encouraging us to help him. Staff Sergeant Laval isn't what I expected out of an RCMP Officer. He's very forthcoming."

"Don't be too sure about him. Laval is a little slippery. He may be telling you what you need to know or maybe he's baiting you to lower your guard around him."

Suzanne noted a twinge of jealousy. Caroline has always been very ambitious and to see a fellow officer climb the ladder faster than her probably irked her.

"Since we're talking about slippery figures, I don't trust Tony," Charles said.

"Adeline's ex-husband?" Carolina asked.

"Yes." He filled Caroline in on the encounter Suzanne had with him earlier in the day. "Suzanne seems a little taken by this well-dressed accountant, but he doesn't fool me. He's too slick."

Suzanne didn't like being accused of being hoodwinked, but she could admit that she wasn't considering Anthony as a prime suspect. "Go on then, let's hear your theory."

"Well for starters, he has motive," Charles said. "He's been paying alimony to Adeline for more than twenty years. By all accounts she was refusing to ever marry again, solely because it would stop her from cashing in on his cheques. He says they had reconciled, but I've never met a man who was happy to be paying alimony."

"Okay, he certainly has a motive," Caroline said. "I've seen my fair share of women murdered by their ex-husbands."

"But what about means?" Suzanne asked. She was keeping an open mind because maybe she had been too easy on this smooth businessman.

"He had a key to Adeline's home," Charles said.

"He admitted it way too easily. Don't you think that if he murdered Adeline, he would have concealed the fact that he had a key to her home? And besides, how would he have broken into our place?" Suzanne asked.

"I don't know." Charles clearly hadn't entirely thought through his notion. He got up and put the kettle on. "He's rich, and he's resourceful. Maybe he figured out a way to do it. Maybe he had help, or … maybe he hired an expert. Either way, I would think that breaking into our house would be a small obstacle for a man like him."

"Perhaps, he got help from Lan?" Caroline said.

Suzanne wasn't sure. But she had to consider it a possibility. Why did all of our theories always involve Lan? All roads pointed back to her.

"Maybe. They do seem to be awfully close." Charles said. "I know what you told me about Gamblers Anon, but they seem closer than just two ex-addicts helping each other out."

"He's her sponsor." Suzanne corrected him. "And if you're making more tea, I'll have some too."

"They're still too chummy, if you ask me." He walked over and retrieved Suzanne's mug. He turned to his daughter and asked, "Can I get you something?"

"Thanks pops, I'm good. But as far as you know, has Lan returned?" Caroline asked.

"No," responded Suzanne.

"When was the last time anyone saw her?"

"Last night," Charles answered. "Should we be worried?"

"I'll go take a look at Adeline's later on. See what I can find. If she doesn't return by nightfall you should contact the RCMP," Caroline advised.

"Thank you," Charles said.

"There is another possibility," Caroline said. "Adeline was your strata treasurer for many years. Maybe someone we haven't even considered killed her for something to do with the strata financing."

"It's possible," Suzanne said. "I did think of it, but if it is the case, then the RCMP are surely combing through the books. They'll find any sign of crooked accounting."

Charles glanced down at his watch and declared, "Oh biscuits, it's almost four-thirty. There's no time for tea. I was supposed to go out with Ivan for a few drinks at the Dockside."

That was the first that Suzanne had heard of this, but she pretended not to let it bother her. The last few days had been long and stressful; She couldn't blame him for wanting to blow off a little steam with his best friend.

As everyone was getting up from the table, Caroline said, "At this point, we also have to assume that we don't have all the pieces of the puzzle. We have just enough to guess at what we're looking at, but we are still just guessing."

Charles hurried out to the pub and Caroline left the room to check her email. Suzanne was left to tidy up alone. She had a smile on her face. She took a sip of her hot tea and poured Charles' down the sink. Regardless of all the possible suspects that they had discussed earlier, she was confident that eventually, with the help of her family, they would soon be besting her arch-rival, Regina Snow.

****

"I hope you had fun," Suzanne said as she opened the front door for her husband. Charles was fumbling with his keys. Unsurprisingly, he had drunk one too many and was having trouble with the new lock.

"I did," he said boisterously. "You missed out on a good time."

"I bet."

"No seriously. I had some interesting company. You'll never guess who I had dinner with." Charles took off his shoes and poured himself a glass of water. It had been his anti-hangover regime from his youth, drink lots of water. He didn't appear to be all-out drunk, but he was boyishly spirited. It was clear that Charles wanted to play his favourite game of making her squirm for information.

Suzanne, on the other hand, wasn't in the mood. "Be quiet, Caroline is asleep in the guest room." The only other bedroom in the townhome was located on the first floor, a few metres from where they stood.

"She's already asleep?"

"It's ten-thirty. You know that she's an earlier riser. She'll get up and run half a marathon before you even open your eyes tomorrow morning."

Suzanne often mocked her husband for regularly sleeping until ten. Back in the day, when he worked in construction, he would've been awake and ready for work an hour before dawn. Post-retirement, he often said that he had many years' worth of sleeping to catch up on. Regardless of Suzanne's jesting, there were very few things in his retired life that Charles enjoyed more than sleeping in.

"Okay come on, guess who I met at The Dockside." He sounded annoyed that she wasn't playing his game.

"Was it Miss Fisher from 105?" Suzanne often kidded that the lonely older lady had eyes for him.

"No, you're not even trying. She'd never step into a pub. Maybe if I were drinking at the opera I'd run into Lizy. But she wouldn't be caught dead at a bar at the end of a marina."

A thought occurred to Suzanne, and she hoped that she was correct. "Was it Lan? Is she alright?" Earlier, she had phoned the RCMP and asked to speak to Staff Sergeant Laval. He wasn't available, nor was he answering his cell. She talked to a clerk and reported that Lan was missing. The clerk asked if Suzanne could come to the police station in the morning. Suzanne wondered if she was over-reacting. But it wasn't like Lan to disappear like this. Even if Suzanne's suspicions were correct and she was off gambling, surely she would have notified someone by now.

"No, sorry it wasn't her. I wish it were." Charles's voice sounded less cheerful. Undoubtedly, he was worried about Lan too. It was no longer time for games. "I met Rob, Murray's stepson."

It took a moment for the information to set in. "Really? What's he like? Tell me everything. Start from the beginning."

"He's actually quite nice." Charles refiled his glass of water and tiptoed into the living room.

Suzanne sat in her chair and instinctively picked up her needlepoint. Charles slumped down onto his sofa. "Rob and Murray never really got along, but there were a few years when they tried. Rob was raised mostly by his real dad. When Murray and Lilith got married, they travelled a lot. We already knew that. And well … they never took Rob with them. His mom always had an excuse for why he couldn't come. His schooling was the biggest reason, which made sense, but even in the summers, he was never invited.

"It was only when Lilith got sick, she had cancer, that she and Murray stayed at home more. Murray was Lilith's sentry and bedside nurse. He stood by her through it all and Rob appreciated that. Sadly, Lilith's cancer kept coming back, and after the third bout of chemo, Lilith said that she was through with treatment. She wanted to enjoy the rest of her life, so she and Murray did what they had always done, they left. Lilith passed away on a cruise ship off the coast of Crete. Rob was really hurt that he wasn't there with his mom when she passed, but at the same time, he knew that it was her final wish.

"For a short while, he and Murray got along. I guess they shared the common bond of mourning for Lilith. But Murray's depression led him straight down the bottle, and the two of them grew apart. Rob was fifteen when he lost his mother. His paternal Father never had a kind word to say about her, so Murray was one of the only people he could talk to about her. Sadly, Murray was drunk most of the time and unable to maintain a meaningful conversation. A few years later, Rob's real Dad remarried, and the family moved to the States. By then Rob and Murray weren't talking any more anyways.

"They hadn't communicated for years, until out of the blue, Murray tracked him down and wrote him a letter. It said that he cleaned himself up. He was a hundred percent sober and in love again. He was planning on proposing and wanted to clear the air between the two of them. Murray explained that he had regretted the way the two of them had fallen apart, and he wanted to be a better stepfather. The new woman was Adeline, of course." Charles took a breather which allowed Suzanne time to process everything.

"I can see where this is going," Suzanne said and signalled him to go on.

"They talked on the phone and stuff for a while. Rob has kids of his own, and he thought it was nice that they might one day meet him. But as we know, Adeline broke off the engagement, and Murray started drinking again. It didn't take long for things to deteriorate between Rob and him again. It's been years since Rob heard from Murray. He didn't even receive Christmas cards. He stopped thinking about his drunken stepdad from BC."

"I never realized that Murray drank that much," Suzanne said.

"We've only known him for a few years. I've seen him tie one on lots of times. But he also maintained his job, so he couldn't have been that bad." Charles answered. His story complete, Charles turned on the TV to watch the late night news.

"I need to call Laval and tell him what happened. Do you think it's too late?" The question was rhetorical; the phone was already in her hand.

"Don't bother," Charles said as he turned the television on. "Who do you think bought the first round?"

"What? Explain yourself." Suzanne hand shot out, grabbed the remote and turned the television off.

Charles seemed perturbed. He should have realized that Suzanne wouldn't let him rest until he told her everything. "Robert may have been mad at his stepfather, but he had also just learned that he had potentially inherited millions of dollars. Apparently, Murray may not have had too much money left in the bank, but he owned dozens of acres of land where his cabin is. It appears a mining company has been trying to buy it from him for years. There are some native land claims, but a representative from the local Native band has already contacted him and is willing to work something out.

"That quickly put Rob into a forgiving mood. He wanted to learn more about his dear departed stepdad. He flew into town and contacted the only person he knew in Sechelt, Staff Sergeant

Laval, who had originally notified him of Murray's passing. Laval was all too happy to show Rob around town and to his stepfather's cabin. After that, Laval offered to treat him to dinner and a few drinks at the Dockside."

"That's an odd thing to do," Suzanne noted.

"I thought so too. Rob had just become a millionaire, you'd think he'd buy the meal," Charles laughed at his own joke, Suzanne didn't. "Well anyways, that's where Ivan and I ran into them. Laval offered to buy us all dinner and a few drinks. I'm not going to say no to a free meal and beer, so I ordered some ribs and told Rob all that I know about Murray. How we've been pals for many years and that Murray was always very nice to us. After that Rob recounted everything that I just told you. I knew you'd want to hear it, so I paid extra close attention."

"Unreal," Suzanne said, more to herself than to Charles. This was the second time in a week in which Charles had found himself in a conversation that she would've very much liked to take part in. Maybe she needed to start going with him to the pub. It was a hub of information.

Chapter

17

Saturday, December 12th, late morning

"**D**o you need me to come into the police station with you?" Caroline asked, her hands firmly on the steering wheel, planted at two and ten o'clock. Suzanne assumed that Caroline didn't usually steer so studiously and was only doing so for her benefit. It was a foggy morning, and Caroline was right to be careful on the road. Even though Suzanne had never had the inclination to drive, she felt the responsibility of ensuring that whoever was driving, did so correctly.

"Don't be silly, dear. You said that you needed to pick up some stuff for your stay. I'm quite capable of filing a missing person's report by myself. Besides, it's the weekend, and I doubt Laval will be there. So you needn't worry."

"Laval is the type of cop that works weekends," Caroline stated.

"We'll see."

The two of them had spent much of the previous evening discussing both the case and its lead investigator. Caroline brought down her laptop and showed Suzanne some of the information which she had uncovered in regards to the young officer. Caroline reminded her, "You can't believe everything the media prints about a person."

Suzanne considered what the newspapers have been saying about her daughter and couldn't hold back a sigh. Still, she was curious as to what had been reported about Laval.

Staff Sergeant Laval had led a very colourful career. Much of it shrouded in mystery. He had been involved in a massive police corruption scandal in Winnipeg. Although he had not been convicted of any crimes, Laval was transferred to Northern Quebec, which pretty much should have been the end of his police career. Instead he received promotion after promotion, before returning to Central Canada. Caroline asserted that it didn't add up. All of which led to further suspicion in regards to the matter that most concerned her: his character. Caroline insisted that Laval's charming demeanour was merely a ploy for Suzanne to keep her guard down as he built his case against her. Suzanne didn't agree.

As predicted, Caroline woke up early and went for a jog, despite the thick fog and light rain. Suzanne sat at the kitchen table, sipped on a strong coffee and waited for her to return. "Do you still like a glass of chocolate milk after your run?"

Caroline smiled. "You remembered." She was only slightly out of breath.

"Some things never change, dear. It's the little things that keep us whole." Suzanne smiled back at her daughter. She was very proud of how her little girl had turned out. Caroline was steadfast and loyal, two excellent qualities for any person. Regardless of any personal matters that may be complicating Caroline's life, she could always be relied upon when needed. She got that from her dad, they were both rocks.

Suzanne made them some breakfast while Caroline showered. The only full bathroom was upstairs beside their bedroom, but there was little risk of waking Charles. He needed to sleep off yesterday's drink, and very little could stop that.

It was during breakfast that the two of them decided to drive into Sechelt. Suzanne wanted to comply with the clerk's request to formally file a missing person's report on Lan and Caroline had a few errands to run.

"Should we wake Dad and tell him we're going into town?" Caroline asked while draining her coffee.

"Are you kidding me? That oaf might sleep until lunchtime. I made him some breakfast and left him a note. He'll be fine."

****

"I'd like to file a report regarding my missing friend, Lan Hynes" Suzanne said to the clerk as she entered. She was relieved to find an empty lobby.

"Just one moment, please," The clerk said in response as she motioned Suzanne to take a seat. The car ride had been murder on her hips, and she opted to stand in the corner. The clerk was a young woman who looked too casually dressed for an administrative assistant within a government office. She wore too much make-up and looked as if she was going to a party. How she can she possibly type with such long fingernails, Suzanne thought. The clerk picked up the phone and made a quick call.

After a very short interval, Suzanne heard a familiar voice beckoning to her, "Hello Ms. Rickson, it's a pleasure to see you again." Staff Sergeant Laval appeared from around the corner clad in a blue suit and a gray tie. Even on the weekends, he dressed professionally.

Suzanne followed Laval down a narrow corridor and was led into his office. "Please come in." He held his door open for her. Laval's office was neat and tidy, just as she expected. He had only occupied it for a short time, but it already had many personal touches. There was an older photo of a young couple on their wedding day. She assumed that they were his parents; a curious choice for a young man's work decor.

Suzanne's gaze was caught by a white orchid by the window sill.

"Do you like it? I bought it the other day," Laval asked.

"It's stunning," she responded.

"I got the idea from you. I noticed you had a few of them. They looked beautiful in your home. I remembered that orchids are low maintenance and the bloom lasts for many months. It's a perfect flower for an office space."

"It'll get too much sun by the south window and burn," Suzanne advised. She scanned the office and looked for a better spot. "I recommend that you leave it on that table there. It'll receive better indirect sunlight."

Laval got up and moved it. "*Merci.*" Suzanne made a mental note the Laval often mixed in a touch of French when speaking to her, and only to her. Was it his way of relating himself to her?

"Don't overwater it. Most orchids die from too much water." Suzanne could've lectured him all day about home gardening, but that wasn't why she was there, so she changed the subject. "I wanted to file an official missing person's report on Lan Hynes."

Laval returned to his seat. "I received a message about that last night and started an investigation right away. I'm afraid that I don't have much information to offer you at this point, other than we've located Ms. Hynes' vehicle."

"Already, that's fantastic!"

"It wouldn't call it fantastic. It was found in the long term parking lot at the ferry terminal. I've inquired with BC Ferries, but at this time I can't confirm that she boarded a vessel."

"Staff Sergeant, have you spoken to Anthony Wong regarding Lan's disappearance?" she asked.

"*Oui,*" Laval said. "He contacted us last evening too. He confided in me the sensitive nature of their relationship."

"Good." Suzanne said. "Then I hope you've contacted all the casinos in Vancouver."

Laval grinned. "Mr. Wong said that you had figured out Lan's little secret. So, I think it's safe to tell you that yes, indeed we have spoken to all the Lower Mainland's casinos. They've assured me that we'd be notified immediately if she enters any of their premises."

"Sadly, I don't think she wants to be found. She won't gamble in Vancouver because she knows that we'd be looking for her there." Suzanne was very much hoping that Lan's disappearance was merely as they had all surmised, that she was relapsing in a casino. For as bad as that was, the alternatives seemed far more grim. Still, she asked, "Staff Sergeant, I need to know, was there any sign that she may not have been travelling alone?"

"At this point, we know very little."

Suzanne sensed something in his voice; he wasn't being entirely forthcoming with all of the information. She didn't pry any further. Instead, she just looked at him with the same look that she used to give her children when she knew that there was something that they weren't telling her.

Surely Laval would be far less susceptible to her powers than her children. Still, after a moment to ponder the situation, he caved in. "Look, I just don't want you to worry too much. The 19:20 ferry two days ago was possibly the ferry that she took to Vancouver. It was forced to make an emergency stop, when several passengers reported hearing a large splash. The ferry doesn't exactly stop on a dime, but safety officials were quickly summoned to the deck and searched for any signs of someone or something in the water. They didn't find anything."

"Was the Coast Guard notified?"

"Yes, but they didn't find anything either. Now as you know, ferry travel to the Mainland is free, and walk-ons to the ferry are only required to provide a free ticket to board. I've spoken to BC Ferries myself, and they know that there were eighteen walk-ons onto that ferry and a hundred twenty riders via the vehicles that boarded. They counted eighteen walk-off passengers but have no way of tallying how many passengers left via their vehicles. Now this isn't certain proof that no one fell off the boat, because someone could have sneaked on or off the ferry via a vehicle. But they have deemed it unlikely. I can't picture a scenario where someone snuck onto the ferry by car, overpowered Lan and threw her overboard. All of which without being seen and then walked off to maintain the headcount of eighteen at arrival."

"She could have jumped on her own volition," Suzanne noted.

"Similar scenario though. Someone would have had to board by car and then walked off to have taken her place during the headcount when departing. I find it highly unlikely"

"But clearly you've considered it a possibility or else you wouldn't have worked it all out in your head." Suzanne closed her eyes and deliberated for a moment. "No, I think I'm with you on this one, it's far more likely that Lan boarded and departed the ferry without incident. The splash that was reported probably wasn't a person."

"*Merci*," Laval said.

Suzanne very much appreciated Staff Sergeant Laval. She knew that she had found a fellow keen intellectual. He could deduce the most likely scenario but was able to keep an open mind to the possibility of other occurrences.

Back at home was a different matter. She knew that everyone didn't share their ability to discern gossip from fact. She was losing the battle in the court of public opinion. Rumours never really die. Even after being disproved, a kernel remains in everyone's thoughts. The tiniest possibility that Charles was having an affair with Adeline was motive enough for Suzanne to harm her. Even though no one was saying anything to her face, Suzanne had already once experienced the agony of being at the tail end of everyone's suspicions, and she knew the signs that it was happening again. Peers were less likely to engage her in conversation. They maintained civility, but very little more. And she could just sense that her every word and actions were being noted and discussed when she wasn't present.

She didn't get this impression from Laval. She truly believed that she wasn't on the top of Laval's suspect list. He knew that she was being framed. Although one small detail always nagged at her, "I have to ask, Staff Sergeant, why have you taken such an active part in this investigation? Aren't you in charge of running this place?"

Laval smiled and pointed to his head. He thickened his French accent. "To exercise my little grey cells."

Suzanne returned the smile. She knew the reference right away. Hercule Poirot. Her intuition was right from the start, Laval considered himself a great detective, and he couldn't resist an interesting case. She gathered her purse and was about to leave when Laval asked, "Ms. Rickson, I know who your daughter is, and I hope that you aren't employing her to gather classified information in regards to this case?"

Suzanne brought her guard up fast. "I would never," she said indignantly.

"I'm glad because I've been reading about her, much as I assume, she is researching me. She'd have told you by now that I very much believe in the integrity of the RCMP. I will do whatever I can to protect it. That includes the security of our confidential information."

"I understand," she said more compliantly.

"Good Ms. Rickson. Please don't get your daughter in any more trouble than she's already in," Laval warned. "I promise to keep you as informed as I can," he added with a warm grin.

"On that note Staff Sergeant, have they completed the autopsy of Murray yet?" she asked, wondering just how obliging he was willing to be.

"I'm afraid it's too early for that. We're not on an American TV show. These things take time."

Laval said. "But I promise to keep you in the loop as soon as I find out."

She believed him.

Chapter

18

Early afternoon

Suzanne emerged from Laval's office to find
Caroline chatting up the front desk clerk. "You
got your chores done fast," she said.

"I only had to pick up a few things."

Looking at the bags, Suzanne figured that
Caroline's sole task was a quick visit to the liquor
store. The 'few things' consisted of vodka and
Caesar mix. Caroline never used to drink, she
thought and then choose not to comment. Her
daughter didn't need to be nagged.

On the car ride home, Caroline asked, "So
was I right?"

"You were about some things." Suzanne
wasn't the type of person to fully admit that
someone else was absolutely correct and that she
was downright wrong. Caroline must be feeling
pretty smug that she had partially conceded.

"Good," Caroline said as she eyed the rearview mirror. "Because I need you to believe me and not overreact to what I'm about to say next."

"Stop gloating, dear."

"It's not gloating, Mom. I need you to be serious." Caroline paused, and Suzanne sat up straight. "I'm pretty sure we're being followed."

"By who?" Suzanne asked and resisted the urge to turn and look for herself. She'd seen enough dramatic movies to know better.

"I'm not sure. I don't recognize the vehicle."

"Aren't you supposed to be good at these sort of situations?"

"It's a dark pick-up truck. I'm fairly certain that it followed us into town, but they've been keeping their distance. The fog isn't helping."

Suzanne couldn't resist any longer. She turned to see her stalker, but she couldn't distinguish anything more than a pair of high beams. They were at least two hundred metres behind them. "How can you tell it's a truck?" she asked.

"They were following us closer when we were in Sechelt. I saw the vehicle up close."

"Could you see who was driving?"

"No, I tried a few times, but they were always smart enough to remain sufficiently away." They were approaching a sharp curve in the highway.

"Now is our chance," Caroline stated. "Do you want me to lose them?"

"No point dear. If they're following us, they already know that we're going home. Slow down after the bend and let's see if we can get a better view of the driver."

"I doubt that'll work, but I'll give it a try." Caroline decelerated immediately after the curve. The women looked back in hope of identifying their follower. As their pursuant turned the corner, they must have caught onto the plan. The pick-up screeched to a halt. Suzanne was sure that it was the same vehicle that was parked outside her home a couple weeks back. It made a U-turn and headed back towards town.

"Do you want me to follow them?" Caroline asked.

"There's no need to, dear. I already know who it is." Suzanne felt her heart rate increase. What was Regina up to?

They got home to find Charles passed out on the couch. His faithful companion was fast asleep, tucked in beside him. Nero raised his head to acknowledge their arrival, but Suzanne quickly quieted him, "Shh… let Daddy sleep. He needs it."

The two women crept upstairs. Caroline explained that she was going to log into her laptop and respond to some personal email, "You should take a nap, Mom. You look tired."

"I'm far too old to take a nap. But I think I'll meditate a bit." Her doctor had once advised her that meditating was an ideal manner of lower one's blood pressure. Good advice she had thought, but Suzanne wasn't about to start wearing Lulu Lemon yoga pants and chanting mantras with a bunch of strangers. Her form of meditation involved sitting in her chair, closing her eyes and listening to her old records. But she didn't want to disturb her husband, so instead she remained upstairs and lay on her bed.

She measured her breathes and tried to forget what had just happened. It was useless. Everything was spiralling out of control. Everyone in her community was slowly turning against her. She had no doubt that if a lesser mind had been in charge of this case, and Laval hadn't inserted himself, she'd have been arrested by now. Breathing exercises weren't helping.

Charles kept a radio beside his bed and luckily the CBC was playing classical music. She concentrated on the melodies and tuned her mind away from the pick-up truck. She stopped worrying about her elevated pulse rate until...

Suzanne woke up from her meditation sometime after four-thirty. Wow, how did that happen? The house was quiet. She went downstairs and found Caroline at the kitchen table reading the newspaper. An extra saucer with a plate over it and a bowl of fresh fruit were placed before an empty seat. "I kept your tea warm," she said to her mother upon first seeing her.

"Where's Charles?"

"You just missed him. He had his tea and took Nero for his afternoon walk." Even with the previous night of excess and the afternoon hangover, everything was still on routine: tea at four and out for a walk with Nero by 4:20.

"Too old to nap, eh," Caroline jested as Suzanne sat down.

"I guess I needed it more than I thought," she said with a yawn.

"You shouldn't push yourself so hard at your age. You need to rest more."

"I hope you live to my age, so you can feel what it's like to be tired after a short stroll. It's not fun." Suzanne stretched out her shoulder. It was sore just from sleeping on it.

"Dad still goes out for a walk twice a day. I don't hear him complaining," Caroline grinned.

"He complains plenty, just not to you." Suzanne took a sip of tea. It was cold, but she continued to drink it anyway.

"Either way, Dad likes getting out." Caroline sounded tired herself. Maybe she should have taken a nap too.

"I used to go with him, you know," Suzanne said. "Until I slipped and hurt my hip. That's Regina's fault too you know."

"I know Mom."

"Charles and Ivan used to do odd jobs around the property. They'd clear the leaves and mow the lawn. They'd get a little money for all their hard work. Not a lot, you understand, but every little bit helped," Suzanne went on. She had recounted this story to her daughters many times in the past and always insisted on telling it again.

"Well, that was until Regina put an end to it. She decided that it was too much work for seniors to be doing. It was dangerous, and we're not covered insurance-wise. If someone got hurt the strata may be held responsible. As if leaf collecting was hazardous. But she decided to sack them and brought in a far more expensive landscaping company. They're loud. Always using those useless wind blowers and just pushing stuff from one side of the property to the other. And they didn't clean the curbs on the day that I slipped last winter. Charles and Ivan would've cleaned it. I told Regina that I was going to sue, but...."

It happened fast. Suzanne's story was interrupted by a car horn. Nero started barking frantically from outside. Both women ran to the front window in the kitchen. Suzanne squinted in hopes our peering through the fog. She caught a glimpse of the rear end of a truck as it veered onto Mercer Street. It was the same dark pick-up truck. "Cursed reckless driver," swore Suzanne. "One day they're going to kill someone."

Suzanne was still cussing when she noticed that Caroline's face was full of dread. She strained her eyes to try and see what her daughter was reacting to. And then she saw him. "Oh God, please no!" Charles was on the ground. He wasn't moving.

They ran out the door still wearing their slippers. Charles was rising up onto his hands, and Nero was licking his face. Luckily he looked alright.

"Don't get up," Caroline warned, "You may have broken something."

"I didn't break anything." Charles fell back down. " I'm okay. Maybe a little bruised is all."

"You could've been killed," Suzanne said.

"Don't exaggerate," Charles said with a puff.

"I'm not exaggerating. There's a killer in our midst."

Charles struggled to get onto his knees. He seemed determined to get back onto his feet. "I didn't notice it come round the corner, but it must've been coming fast. It could've hit me, but it blew its horn at the last second, and I jumped out of the way."

He looked pale. Suzanne grabbed his wrist to feel his pulse. Charles' heart was racing at a perilous pace.

People were starting to come out of their homes. Even Miss Fisher appeared. Everyone looked concerned. From the corner of her eye, Suzanne spotted Regina standing in the crowd. "What happened," she heard her nemesis say.

"You know what happened? Your son tried to kill my Charles. He nearly ran him over."

"No," Charles objected. "No one tried to kill me."

Suzanne went off on a tirade. "Just because he didn't kill you, doesn't mean he didn't try." She turned back to Regina and stuck her finger right in her face. "You threatened to poison us, and now your son has tried to run my husband over. You don't think I noticed him tailing us this morning. You're trying to kill anyone who's standing up to you. You're crazy and sadistic. I know it was your son, and I'm going to prove it."

"My son is in Alaska," Regina calmly said. "He's been on a fishing boat for the past three weeks. His truck is parked at home in Vancouver. You can call his wife and ask her if you like. The police already have.

The crowd took a collective gasp. They must've all been anticipating this confrontation. It was inevitable.

"I know that you're behind all of this," retorted Suzanne.

More people were arriving. They were all bearing witness to Suzanne and Regina finally having it out.

"It's just like you," Regina countered. "You're always accusing people of being out to get you. I told you already. It wasn't my son. It wasn't him today, and it wasn't his truck you saw before Adeline was murdered. It couldn't have been. The police have confirmed all of this. But you keep spouting your mouth off. I'll tell you again, I had nothing to do with any of this."

Suzanne felt Charles' hand squeeze hers. His eyes were pleading to her to stop. She looked around at the crowd. They were starting to jeer. Someone held up a cell phone. All of a sudden, she realized that she was digging herself deeper and deeper into a hole. Regina had orchestrated all of this, and she was playing right into her trap.

Connie and Ivan appeared by their side. Ivan took Nero's leash, and Connie addressed the crowd, "Show's over folks. You can all go home now."

The onlookers looked disappointed.

"Come on dear, let's go home." Charles pulled Suzanne towards their abode.

"Are you sure you can walk, Dad?" Caroline asked.

"Yes, I'm sure. Just get us home."

Chapter
19

Sunday, December 13th, late morning

The thick fog from yesterday did nothing but intensify overnight. It encompassed everything and created an eerily calm atmosphere. Still, it was not enough to discourage the Sunday group from missing noon mass. They gathered outside, in front of Connie and Ivan's driveway, just as they always did. It did not escape Suzanne that the killer often broke into their townhomes while everyone was at church. It made her feel an awful lot better that Caroline had agreed to stay home and guard the premise.

Charles had a large bruise on his left hip, and his knees were sore. He had hinted earlier to Suzanne that he was too painful for church. She gave him the look, and he gingerly got dressed. With his usual good-humoured tone he greeted Dariya as she arrived, "No Walter today?"

"When was the last time he showed up?" she said.

"Before NFL football season started," Charles joked.

"Walter says that he prays plenty whenever the Seattle Seahawks are playing," Dariya said. There was a time that Walter came to church every week, but about a year and a half ago the excuses started. Now he only showed up for special events.

"I guess we can take one car now," Ivan remarked.

"I think you're right," said Charles. Suzanne didn't say a word. Adeline had always refused to cram into one vehicle, even though they could've all fit into Ivan's Sedona. It always annoyed the rest of them that they had to take two cars just to accommodate her.

The ride into Sechelt was lively, but they all refused to bring up any of their recent troubles. Adeline's, Murray's and Lan's names were never mentioned. No one brought up the events from the day before. Instead, they talked about their Christmas plans. Everyone was looking forward to spending time with their grandchildren. A debate erupted as to how spoiled children were today with their gadgets and video games.

"My daughter, Lisa, told her kids that Santa didn't bring electronics," Suzanne said.

"Oh, that's a good idea," Dariya agreed. They

all laughed. It was precisely what all of them needed, a short term distraction.

They were all in good spirits upon arriving at Our Lady of Lourdes Church. "It doesn't look like many people showed up for mass today," Connie said while scanning for friendly faces.

"It's the fog, sweetie," Ivan said. "Some folks just don't like driving in it."

"More likely people are too busy with last minute shopping and preparing for Christmas," Dariya said.

"The Hendersons left yesterday for Florida. Some people like to get out early, while airlines rates are a little cheaper," Suzanne said.

"A lot cheaper," Charles pointed out. "Our son-in-law is paying a small fortune to fly us all back to Montreal in a few days."

"Oh, is it alright for you guys to leave town?" Dariya asked.

"Why wouldn't it be?" Suzanne said. Without another word, she headed into the church.

Charles followed her. "We'll see you all inside."

Father O'Brian's sermon was about forgiveness. He talked about how Jesus turned the other cheek and quoted from Mark 11-25, "And when you stand praying, if you hold anything against anyone, forgive him, so that your Father in heaven may forgive you your sins."

Suzanne wondered if he was addressing her directly. Could she fully forgive the person who murdered Adeline? She had to be honest with herself. She already knew that the answer was no. She remained in a spiritual crisis for the rest of the service. Even afterwards, as everyone was leaving and Father O'Brian stood in the doorway, shaking everyone's hands as they departed, Suzanne's mind was a flutter.

"I trust you enjoyed today's sermon," he said as he took her hand and peered into her eyes. "I hope it helped," he added.

"Yes, Father, it did," she lied, vowing to confess her little transgression on a future date.

She remained silent as they travelled home. The heater was at full blast, quickly warming the interior. Ivan drove slowly because it was still quite foggy.

"It seems even thicker," Connie said nervously.

"It's perhaps the heaviest fog I've ever seen," Dariya said, sounding even more on edge.

"I've been in thicker," Ivan said. "Once, when I was still in the Navy, we were sailing the Adriatic Sea off the coast of the former Yugoslavia. The fog was so heavy we couldn't see our own boots. You could almost choke on it. This is nothing." He sounded confident in his driving skills. His calm voice seemed to relax his passengers, but only by a little.

Suzanne usually would have been in cahoots with her friends as they fretted in the back seat, but she was still in deep thought until she uncovered her solution. After the hand of justice has adequately punished the evildoers, she would be able to forgive them. But only after that, Lord. You can't ask me to do it before then.

"What was that?" Ivan asked.

"Nothing," Suzanne responded. "Just keep your eyes on the road."

****

The phone rang just after four PM. The Ricksons had just sat down to have tea. "I'll get it," Suzanne said.

"Ms. Rickson. Great, I'm so glad to have caught you."

"Staff Sergeant Laval, don't tell me that you're still at work."

"I'm almost done for the day. I just wanted to ensure that Mr. Rickson was alright?"

"He's a little sore, but he'll be fine." Suzanne had called Laval after mass. She had filled him in on every detail, including her altercation with Regina. He had said very little in return and didn't sound surprised. Suzanne assumed it was because someone had already notified him of the incident. "Surely Staff Sergeant, you didn't just call this late on a Sunday to ask about how Charles was doing. Have you discovered anything about the vehicle?"

"I'm afraid not, Ms. Rickson. Although I can confirm for you that everything Ms. Snow said about her son being in Alaska is true."

"I had to assume it was," Suzanne said. "I was just hoping it wasn't."

"I need to ask you for a favour, Ms. Rickson." Laval's voice sounded a tad hesitant.

What on earth would Laval need from me, she wondered. Nonetheless she responded, "I'll help you any way I can."

"*Merci.* And… oh yes, first I have some news for you. Ms. Hynes is in Las Vegas."

"Oh thank goodness." It wasn't the best of news. It confirmed that Lan had totally digressed. But at least she was alive.

"To be more accurate, I should say that we know she *was* in Las Vegas. I can confirm that she boarded a plane headed to Nevada, early Friday morning. She went through customs and rented a car. I'm not certain she stayed in Las Vegas. All of the larger hotels have said that no one of the name Lan Hynes has checked in. There has been no activity on her credit cards other than for the car rental. If she doesn't want to be found, it is likely that she has checked into a smaller hotel and paid cash."

"I'm just happy she's still among the living," Suzanne said.

"Me too."

"So after such eventful news, please tell me Staff Sergeant, how can I be of help?"

"Well you see, we've searched Ms. Hynes' residence, and it doesn't appear as though any luggage is missing. The airline has confirmed that she brought along a small piece of luggage, which she stored in the overhead bin. Now it's probably nothing, but I like knowing everything. I remember hearing that she often stayed at Ms. Wong's home. Do you suppose that Ms. Hynes would have taken her luggage?"

"It's possible. Adeline had some absurdly expensive designer suitcases."

"I hope it's not too much to ask, but could you go to Ms. Wong's and verify if her luggage is missing... sorry, you know what, it's silly. Forget I called, I'm sorry that I asked."

An odd request, perhaps it's a ploy to gain her trust. "I'd be happy to check it for you. I have to admit that I'm a little curious myself."

They agreed that she'd phone him back from Adeline's home. She decided to take Nero along with her. He'd like that.

Charles and Caroline offered to escort her, but she declined, "I'm not so old that I need your help with everything. Besides, Nero will protect me. Won't you boy?" The dog panted, and she left before they had any time to insist.

Outside was dark and damp. The fog had finally dissipated, but the sun had just sunk back below the horizon. At least it wasn't raining. Suzanne hurried as fast as she could for she didn't want to overly expose herself to the frigid air. So far this winter she had avoided getting a cold or flu, and she planned to keep it that way.

The inside of Adeline's home was almost as cold as it was outside. The heat had been turned off. There was a smell of wilted flowers. Lan had left the roses unattended for far too long. Otherwise, the home was immaculate, just as Adeline had always kept it.

Nero appeared excited to be in the home which he had never been allowed into before. He sniffed in the new environment and seemed anxious to explore. "Stay," Suzanne ordered.

Suzanne couldn't help but empty the flower vase and throw the old bouquet into a plastic bag. She'd carry it home with her and dispose of them in the own trash. She went upstairs and continued her task of searching through Adeline's closet. It didn't take long to discover a significant gap in the luggage set that was neatly stacked in the guest bedroom. Mystery solved, Lan had borrowed Adeline's Louise Vitton for her Vegas trip.

"Hello Staff Sergeant, its Suzanne," she spoke into Adeline's phone.

"Thank you for getting back to me so quickly," he said.

"You were right. Lan has taken Adeline's luggage."

"Technically, the luggage belongs to Lan now, anyways," Laval said.

"True. I just haven't brought myself around to thinking that way yet. It's been two weeks, and I still feel that this all belongs to Adeline."

"These things take time, Ms. Rickson. Trust me, I know."

Something seemed peculiar to Suzanne, but she wasn't sure what. She scanned the living room for any hint of anything out of place, but couldn't find anything. Perhaps the whole scenario was staged. Was she supposed to see something here?

Suzanne found Nero a few feet from where she left him. She grabbed her cane and the garbage bag and left. A thought occurred to her as she turned the key to re-lock the door. How did Laval know that she had access to Adeline's home? Was that the real detail which he really wanted to know: if she had access to Adeline's abode? She didn't have long to analyze it.

****

"Don't get cheeky with me! I know what you did!"

Dariya was practically screaming from the other side of the shrubbery that partitioned Adeline's and her property.

"Stop talking so loud."

It took a second for Suzanne to recognize Regina's voice. She had missed the first half of their argument, but Suzanne made a quick decision to stay and eavesdrop on the rest of it. "Shh," she whispered to Nero.

"Don't try denying it," Dariya said at a slightly lower volume. "I know everything."

"I have no idea what you're going on about."

"I know that you killed Adeline."

"I would never do something like that."

"I know you did it and I know how. You have a master key to all our homes. You used it to go into Adeline's home while she was at church."

"What? I don't have a key to everyone's home. It's just more fiction which you've made up. You read too much, Dariya. Now you're mixing up your novels with real life."

"Oh stop it. Don't patronize me," Dariya shouted. "Two years ago you bragged to Walter and me that you had a master key. You could access anyone's suite, as long as they still had the manufacturer's original locks on their front doors. You said that it was a security measure and that we shouldn't tell anyone about it."

"You're making all that up," Regina's voice changed, there was a hint of desperation in her speech. "No one would believe you if you told them that."

"I wouldn't be so sure. The only way to find out would be to tell them. So let's do that. I know a few people who'd find it very incriminating. I bet that young detective would love to know about your little secret."

"Tell them anything you want. No one will ever find this make-believe key. It won't be there by the time they search my home."

There was a large thump. Dariya must have slammed her door on Regina's face. The sudden noise made Nero bark.

"Who's there?" Regina asked. "Wait... I'd know that annoying bark anywhere. Chuck? Suzy? Is that you?"

Suzanne dropped the garbage bag and started running as soon as Nero barked. She was turning the corner and rounding the back before Regina finished her sentence. She hadn't moved so fast in many years. Her hip was hurting already, but she didn't want to get caught.

It wouldn't be the most pleasant of treks, but Suzanne knew that she could reach her home from the rear of the Building C. Overgrown blackberry bushes littered the empty space that had been reserved for future development. Although it was a harsh and dangerous route, it did have the benefit of being unlit. During past strata meetings Suzanne had often argued with Regina that they should install lights back there for security purposes at night. For the first time ever, Suzanne was glad that she had lost a debate with Regina.

Her feet sank into the mud. Visibility was nil. Suzanne's left sleeve got snagged on a branch full of thorns. "Biscuits," she quoted Charles' favourite cuss word. She was fond of the coat. It had been a Christmas present from Lisa. In any other circumstance she would have delicately pried the thorn out to minimize the damage. Instead Suzanne yanked her arm free and heard the fabric rip.She dropped her cane and fumbled to retrieve it, cutting her hand. Nero howled. He looked up at her as if she had lost her mind.

"I know you're out there." Regina hollered, her voice was close behind. "And I know where you're going. See you soon."

Suzanne and Nero cleared the blackberry bushes. She scanned the road for any sign of Regina. Nothing yet. They arrived home and found the front door to be unlocked. Finally, some good luck. She took off her boots and threw her coat into the closet.

"What's going on?" Charles inquired, clearly perturbed with Suzanne's haste.

"Regina is about to knock on our door. I need you to say that I was here with you all along." She grabbed a dishtowel and wrapped up her hand to stop the bleeding. She tried to control her breathing, but she was exhausted.

"What have you been up to? Are you hurt?" Caroline asked as she scrambled down the stairs.

"I'll explain everything later. There's no time now. Did you hear what I told your Dad?"

"Yes." Caroline knew to obey.

"Is supper ready?" Suzanne asked, noticing that the table was set. She took a seat and rubbed her knees.

"Almost," Charles answered.

"Good. Serve it."

"But..." Charles said, before being interrupted by the doorbell rang. Nero barked once.

"Caroline, be a dear and get that," Suzanne said. "And remember; just go with what I say."

Caroline nodded and opened the door. "Why, hello Mrs. Snow."

Suzanne knew that Regina wasn't one to act overtly. If she suspected that she had been snooped on, Regina would confront whoever she suspected without hesitation or courtesy. She stepped past Caroline and leered at Suzanne.

"Was it you who was spying on me or was it Charles?"

"I have no idea what you are talking about. We were just about to sit down for dinner," Suzanne responded.

Regina scanned the set table and Charles with a colander of steaming noodles. She looked down and eyed Suzanne's swathed up hand. And then her gaze settled on the muddy boots on the mat. "Are you sure that you weren't just out walking your dog?"

Charles answered first, "No, I took him out earlier, before the sun went down."

"I went along with him but that probably about an hour ago," Suzanne added. "Is something wrong?"

"You're holding a bloody towel," Regina said.

"Ahh, it's nothing." Suzanne waved her good hand in the air.

"Save it. Like I'd ever get the truth from you people."

"I feel the exact same way about you," Suzanne countered. "Now if you don't mind, as I said before, we were just about to eat supper." Caroline escorted Regina out.

"Alright, tell us what that was all about?" Charles said while serving spaghetti al dente.

Suzanne took a deep breath and told them everything.

"So why don't you want Regina to know that you overheard her? Dariya said she was going to tell everyone anyway."

"I remembered something Adeline once told me. You mustn't allow your rivals to know when you have the upper hand.

Chapter

20

Monday, December 14th, morning

Suzanne woke up early. In actuality, she never completely fell asleep. Her head was too full of possibilities and strategies. She heard Caroline get dressed and slip out for her morning jog at 5:45. Suzanne couldn't see any reason to stay in bed.

She made herself a cup of coffee and turned on the news. There was a story about Caroline. The Independent Investigations Office of BC hadn't yet completed its review of the incident, but a leak from within hinted that a formal criminal investigation would be recommended. The media was calling Caroline a vigilante. No wonder she's been hiding out in Halfmoon Bay; far away from the scrutiny of the press.

Suzanne wished that her daughter would open up to her and talk about her emotional state. There was a time when the two of them were close. The two tours in Afghanistan altered her. War had a way of changing people. It had altered her father, and now it was affecting her daughter. Soldiers tend to internalize their feelings and shut everyone else out. If Caroline ever wanted to talk about it, she would be there for her. Suzanne felt that perhaps she was being rude by obsessing about her own dilemmas, while her daughter was dealing with some serious issues. But it was painfully clear that Caroline wanted nothing more than a distraction and a quaint little mystery seemed to be doing the trick.

Last night had been another late night. The three of them had sat in the living room and discussed everything concerning their case. Charles thought that they should inform the authorities about the argument that Suzanne had eavesdropped on.

"Because I can't prove anything," she explained. "Besides, if I know Dariya, it will all be common knowledge very soon."

Caroline and Charles seemed content to leave the next move up to Suzanne, and they went to bed at midnight. Suzanne remained in her chair and closed her eyes. Regina would strike soon. Suzanne had Regina backed into a corner, but much like a wild animal, that's when they're the most dangerous.

So perhaps the wisest thing to do is to not threaten Regina. Much like Adeline had once tried to teach her in Mahjong. The art of setting a trap relies on the prey not knowing that they are being hunted. She needed to instil upon Regina a false sense of confidence.

She went to bed with that sole approach in mind, but she still couldn't sleep. There were too many variables. Dariya was too unpredictable. Her big mouth won't stay shut for long. So Regina will have to act quickly.

Suzanne was convinced that Regina was behind the attempted murder of her husband. She pondered as to why the driver honked the horn and didn't hit Charles. If it was the killer that was driving the vehicle, why not run his victim over? If it wasn't Regina's son behind the wheel, then who was it? Byron perhaps? Maybe that's why he honked. Byron couldn't hurt anyone, even if Regina had ordered him to do so.

Perhaps the entire plot was meant to be a charade; a clever ruse to cloud everyone's judgment. It was the most likely scenario. This is all just a battle between her and Regina. Her nemesis was using everyone else as pawns to be sacrificed. Adeline's murder had been perpetrated solely for the purpose of framing her. The fake attempt on Charles' life was entirely aimed at scandalizing her. Regina has to be stopped before more people get hurt. But how? That's the question that had kept Suzanne awake all night.

By ten AM Caroline had still not returned. Suzanne knew not to worry about her. Caroline was a strong runner, and if she had something on her mind, she was liable run the length of a double marathon. She might not be back until midday. Charles had woken and ate breakfast. The two of them had a quiet chat before he left for his morning stroll with Nero. "Do you want to come with us," he offered.

"No, my hip hurts like a son of a gun." She had overexerted herself last night. She had so many cuts and scrapes that she had run out of Band-Aids.

"Rest then," Charles said gently. He seemed quite stiff himself, but that wouldn't deter him from his morning routine.

"I will," Suzanne answered.

The house was all quiet again.

Something else had kept Suzanne up the night before. There was another problem that lingered in her subconscious. Perhaps it was a less urgent dilemma, but nonetheless, it needed to be attended to. If Regina was a situation best left to see what would happen next, her other problem demanded action. Suzanne decided that now was the time to act.

It had been over a week since she had spoken with Lisa, which was very uncommon. Lisa was obviously upset, and Suzanne felt responsible for rectifying it.

A stereotypical Canadian says the word 'sorry' at least ten times a day. Not Suzanne, she tried to avoid using that word. She couldn't remember the last time she had said it to one of her daughters, but maybe this time it was needed. She picked up the phone and dialled Lisa's number. She fully intended to apologize for the outburst and judgment that she had cast on their last conversation. It wasn't her place to interfere with Lisa and Mark's relationship. As much as her intentions were good, perhaps she came off a little too opinionated. She figured, just like with a band-aid, she should blurt out the word fast and quickly and not dwell on it. That may have been her intention, but something else happened instead.

"How are you, dear?" Suzanne asked in a gentle voice.

"Tired."

"The kids keeping you up?"

"No, the boys are sweet," Lisa responded and hesitated for a moment. "It's Mark and me. We've been arguing. You were right Mom. He's working longer and longer hours and doesn't prioritize any time for his family."

Now this was unexpected. As much as Suzanne rarely said the word 'sorry', Lisa had never before uttered the words, "you were right,

Mom."

"You said last time that it was just this trial. It was big and demanded a lot of his attention," Suzanne said.

"After this big trial, there'll be another one. Lawyers measure their success by how many hours they bill. And that's the only thing Mark cares about, success."

"I'm sure you're exaggerating. He loves you and the kids."

"Maybe, but he loves his career more. He pretty much admitted it to me last night."

"Did he say it while you two were arguing, dear? Men say all sorts of crazy things when they're angry."

"We weren't fighting. We were discussing things like rational adults. That's what hurts more. He said it coldly and intentionally. The man loves his job more than he loves me."

"I don't know what to say, dear."

"And I don't know what to do." Lisa sounded desperate. How can this be? Last week she was defending this man. Her daughter could be so overly dramatic. "Oh, and there's another thing. Mark's not coming to Montreal with us. He's too busy. Who's busy at Christmas? Maybe he'll make it there after the 25th. Yeah right!"

That wasn't surprising at all, Suzanne thought. This wasn't the first time he had pulled out of a family vacation. He probably likes the quiet house. Everyone except Lisa had already assumed that he was going to do it again this year. Still, Suzanne responded, "That's a pity, dear. We were all hoping that he could make it this time."

"Give it a break, Mom. I know that you never liked him."

There's no point in blatantly lying. Lisa would see right through it. Suzanne opted to admit the truth and spin it as well as she could. "We may not always see eye to eye, but Mark has always been a very well-mannered young man and provides for his family. And as much as I think he loves making money too much, he has always been very generous with it."

"Being generous and well-spoken doesn't make for a great dad. You said it yourself last week."

"I'm sorry, dear. I was out of place." There she said it. "And you were right too. Mark hasn't changed. He's the same man you fell in love with and married. You're an excellent mother, and it more than compensates for Mark not always being there. Trust me, he's a good man, and he'll be there when you need him."

"I don't know, Mom." Lisa sounded as though she was about to cry.

Just then the front door opened. "Speaking of good men, mine just walked in. And he's drenched. Do you want to say hello?"

"No, it's okay. You go take care of Dad, and I'll call you back later."

"Sure. Are you okay?"

"I will be. And thanks, Mom."

"You're welcome." She may have poured it on a bit thick there at the end. But Lisa believed it, and that's all that mattered.

****

Suzanne and Charles had just sat down to eat lunch when they spotted Caroline through their kitchen window. Their daughter seemed impervious to the rain as she stretched out her muscles during her post-run routine.

"Do you remember when we used to be able to bend like that?" Charles said.

"I don't even remember bending at all. It seems like such a long time ago."

When Caroline finally came in, she announced that she was going to take a shower.

"We made you a corned beef sandwich and a tall glass of chocolate milk," Charles offered.

"Thanks," she said, grabbed the milk and walked upstairs.

"Kids," Charles remarked. "They never grow up."

Suzanne kept eating her soup. There was too much on her mind to engage in banter. Charles had been trained a long time ago that when Suzanne wanted silence, it was best to give it to her. They ate the remainder of their meal without saying a word.

Sirens broke the quiet.

Oh no, not again. Suzanne strained her ears. "Two ambulances," she said.

"Are you sure?"

Instead of answering Suzanne just leered at him.

"But why two ambulances?" he asked.

It was a silly question that was rhetorical in nature. The answer was not spoken between them. Two ambulances for two people. But for whom?

The Ricksons watched from their window as they raced by, around the bend, towards Building C.

"Get dressed," Suzanne said.

Charles put his shoes on and retrieved the leash. Nero was getting excited. Upstairs the water was still running. Caroline was warming her cold body in a hot shower. "We'll leave her a note," Charles suggested.

It was chilly and wet. The rain wasn't letting up and continued to beat down on the coast. It was too windy for an umbrella, which suited Suzanne fine. She hated holding an umbrella. She considered them more as sails than a device to stay dry. A warm coat with a sturdy hood is always better suited for West Coast storms.

All three of them made their way up the road. The tiny dog whimpered.

They turned the corner and spotted the two ambulances stopped near the end of the new townhomes.

Oh, please be for Regina, Suzanne thought. The alternative wouldn't be good.

Sadly for her, it was the alternative. Regina and Byron were among the bystanders that were standing outside of Walter and Dariya's home. The Ricksons arrived just as the paramedics were carrying Dariya's inert body out on a gurney. Her skin looked extremely pale. Another pair of attendants were trying to cox Walter into lying still on his stretcher. He appeared to be hyperventilating, but he was also lively and animated. His arms were flailing as if he were punching the air. Everyone watched as the paramedics struggled to get him into the back of their ambulance. He was shouting that he wanted to be with his wife. Walter's eyes caught Suzanne's, and he shouted, "You did this."

Regina turned almost as if on cue. "What? Did you poison them too?"

"I didn't poison anyone. It was you."

Regina ignored Suzanne's counter-accusation. "First you poisoned Adeline for sleeping with Charles, and now you've poisoned sweet Dariya.

Why? Because she ratted you out about the library book that you took out."

Regina had caught everyone's attention. They were all watching the spectacle. Round two. Regina continued her performance, "You know, the library book about homemade poisons. The one you borrowed two weeks before Adeline was killed. And now you've poisoned Dariya and Walter. You're a cold-blooded killer who's silencing all your loose ends."

"A loose end isn't someone who has already defamed you." Suzanne proclaimed. Charles grabbed her hand and squeezed it tight. Suzanne ignored him.

"Fine, I'm not as brushed up on criminal lingo as you. It was for revenge then. You poisoned Dariya because she spread rumours about you. Well then, I guess we all better keep our mouths shut around you or you might just kill us all."

Suzanne felt Charles tugging on her whole arm. She pulled herself free. There was no going back now. "It's more likely you killed Adeline. You knew she was going to beat you in the elections. No matter what you claim, she was going to win."

"I've told you already, I had enough proxy votes to win easily."

"Has anyone seen all these phantom proxy votes that you claim to have?" Suzanne fired back.

"I don't have to show you anything. Just ask half the people here, and they'll tell you, they had already voted for me."

"Probably because you bullied them into it."

"What? Are we name calling now?" Regina sneered. "You think I'm a bully? You're a miserable old hag. It doesn't matter how I got their vote. All that matters is that I did. So there goes your theory on my motive. Your motivation, on the other hand, is the oldest in the book. You killed Adeline for seducing your husband."

The crowd hissed at that comment. Suzanne was just about to lose her temper, but she took a deep breath instead of shouting out her denial. It was Charles who couldn't hold his tongue, "How dare you say such things. The rumour of Adeline and me was completely made up by you to slander us during the last election."

"See there you're wrong," Byron spoke for the first time. "It was Dariya who once saw the two of you together and started talking about your possible relationship with Adeline. So there's yet another reason for you to have poisoned poor Dariya. You're both crazy and paranoid. Like mad dogs. You need to be stopped."

Charles was livid. He clenched his fists and advanced upon Byron. The onlookers gawked. Suzanne ran as fast as she could to stand in front of Charles and block his path. His eyes were enraged. She caught his gaze and whispered, "Enough."

Charles broke down immediately. Suzanne watched as the anger washed away from his face leaving a look of

confusion. It was as if he didn't know where he was anymore.

A police car pulled up in front of them. The RCMP had finally arrived. The tension in the air broke immediately, as no one wanted to appear remotely guilty of anything. Corporal Bridges stepped out of the car and proceeded directly inside the townhome. Staff Sergeant Laval emerged and quickly spoke with the paramedics before they whisked their patients away; sirens blaring from the get-go.

Laval looked displeased and yet still very focused. He walked straight up to Suzanne. "Ms. Rickson." He nodded in salutation.

She didn't waste time with pleasantries, "What's happening, Staff Sergeant?"

"The paramedics think that they ingested something. They arrived to find Ms. Underhill unconscious and Mr. Underhill appearing to be extremely intoxicated. I've been told he's quite the alcoholic."

"He's not that bad," Regina inserted herself into the conversation. "He's been my neighbour for many years, and I've never seen him drunk in the morning before."

"It was he that phoned 911. He had claimed that they both got very sick soon after breakfast. They were vomiting profusely," Staff Sergeant Laval informed them.

"Dariya has bad kidneys," Charles said.

"She has chronic kidney disease," Suzanne informed them. "I believe she was taking medication for it and that it was under control. It will surely complicate matters." She always found it ironic that it was Dariya who had kidney disease when it was Walter who drank like a fish.

"Can we go to the hospital?" Regina asked. She appeared to be sincerely concerned for the wellbeing of her neighbours, but she was a master at feigning empathy.

"I'd rather none of you did. Their family will be there, and I'd appreciate it if we didn't bring any drama to the hospital right now."

"We understand," Byron said, holding his wife.

Laval turned directly to Suzanne and said, "I'll keep you informed of any changes." Suzanne appreciated it.

Connie and Ivan appeared from behind them and asked, "What the heck is going on?"

"It's Dariya and Walter. They've been taken

to the hospital," Charles answered.

"Dear God, not again?" Connie asked.

"God had nothing to do with this. It was Regina." Suzanne said.

Charles massaged the back of his neck. "What took you guys so long to get here? You're usually the first people to arrive at these sort of things?"

"We had to get dressed. We were in bed," Ivan responded.

"It's past noon, and you were still asleep?" Charles asked.

Ivan just winked.

Chapter
21

Late morning

The Ricksons took turns explaining the morning's affairs to Connie and Ivan as they strolled back home. The Heslops gasped and chuckled as they were told the details of the verbal battle with the Snows.

"You should have slugged him," Ivan said.

"Whatever happened to turning the other cheek?" Suzanne asked.

"Even our Lord Saviour, Jesus Christ, would have smacked Byron for that comment."

"Blasphemy, Ivan?" Suzanne chastised.

"Bah, he's heard it all before."

Caroline was at the kitchen table eating a bowl of cereal when her parents returned. "What was all the fuss about?" she asked.

They caught her up to speed, but Caroline seemed distracted. When they finished, Caroline offered no personal insight. Instead she said, "I have to go back to Vancouver."

"I know," Suzanne said.

"I'm catching the 2:20 ferry, but I'll be back as soon as I can. I have to go pack. Are you going to be alright without me?"

"Things are almost settled here, dear. I'll talk to Laval later today, and it should be done. Thanks for all your help," Suzanne said.

Caroline offered no other detail as to why she has to leave, but Suzanne knew that it was tied into the news story she had heard earlier in the morning. She had lied when she told her daughter not to worry about them, that they'd be alright without her. The truth was that both she and Charles were going to miss her. They both felt much safer while their ex-soldier / police officer daughter was in the house.

As soon as Caroline left the kitchen Charles asked, "How did you calm down so fast when Regina and Byron were attacking us?"

"Isn't it you who says that if you lose your temper, you've already lost?"

"True… but under the circumstances. They accused you of killing Adeline."

"And don't you also preach that it is important to know your enemy?"

"Enough with all the smart things I say, what was going on?"

"Two things," Suzanne said as she sat down. "One, the obvious, Regina overheard Walter accuse me of poisoning him. And being who she is, she took the opportunity to confront us."

"I get that," Charles said as took a bite of his lunch.

"But what's important to note is that it very much appeared to be impromptu. She poisoned the two of them in order to silence Dariya, but she couldn't have anticipated Walter being conscious and blaming me. She hadn't planned on verbally battling us today."

"Okay, I'll buy that. What's your second point?"

"On top of being an opportunist, Regina wouldn't have confronted me publically, unless she had an ulterior motive. I'm certain that she was behind the pick-up truck incident. It was carefully orchestrated to discredit us. But today it was different." Suzanne paused for dramatic effect, just like they did in her favourite novels. "She was fishing. Regina is still unsure if I had overheard her conversation last night."

"Is that still important?"

"Well for starters, it will help her decide if she needs to murder us or not."

"Us?" Charles coughed out a mouthful of sandwich.

"She'll assume that I've told you everything. Which of course I did. So you'll have to be killed too."

"So then, shouldn't we be acting soon? Shouldn't we go to the police with what we know?"

"I've almost figured everything out. But just because I know the truth, it doesn't mean that I can prove it. And there are still a few holes that I need to fill."

"So what's next then?" Charles asked, regaining his composure.

"You guard the house, and I'm going to catch a ride with Caroline. I need to get some coffee."

****

Anthony Wong had agreed to meet Suzanne during working hours, as long as it was close to his job. They settled on a quaint café in Sechelt.

"Thank you for meeting me under such short notice," she said.

"It's always a pleasure, Mrs. Rickson. Sorry..." he said with a nod of his head. "I mean Suzanne."

"The pleasure is all mine. And thank you again for the coffee." Anthony had insisted on buying the beverages; a true gentleman, just like

Lan had once described him.

"I have to admit, I was just about to call you too." Anthony flashed his smile.

"Really," Suzanne said and took a small sip to test the coffee's temperature. Way too hot. These fancy coffee shops always make their drinks too hot.

"I wanted to tell you that I was going to Vegas - to find Lan," Anthony said.

Suzanne wasn't surprised. He was after all Lan's sponsor, and as such, he felt responsible for her wellbeing. "Are you going to bring her back?"

"I'm going to try."

"Your wife doesn't mind," Suzanne asked, for no other reason than curiosity.

"She understands." The heat of the coffee didn't seem to bother Anthony, he swallowed a large gulp.

"Actually it was Lan I was hoping to talk to you about. I needed to ask you a few questions. Do you mind?"

"I hope you can understand, Suzanne, some things between her and me are confidential. I can't betray her trust."

"I'll try not to put you on the spot," Suzanne said. "It's nothing to do with her gambling. At least…I hope not."

"Well, then ask your questions and I'll be as accommodating as I can."

"Thank you," Suzanne said, praying that he would opt to tell the truth and she wouldn't be lying awake all night trying to decipher the facts from his lies. "First off, do you remember that ring we once talked about?"

"Murray's engagement ring to Adeline?"

"Yes, exactly. Did you ever find out what happened to it, after you sold it back to him?"

"I told you before I have no clue or claim to it."

Anthony was already sounding defensive, which wasn't what Suzanne wanted. She decided to tread a tad lighter. "I believe you. It's what he did afterwards that I'm trying to figure out."

"We already discussed this. He probably had it with him when he committed suicide, and it washed away." Anthony speculated.

"Yes, it's completely possible. But it's Lan's behaviour that concerns me. You see, just after Adeline died, I found Lan frantically searching for it. Lan had assumed that Adeline still had it. No doubt she was learning that Adeline was nowhere near as wealthy as everyone thought. But at least she'd inherit the ring."

"That makes sense," Anthony agreed.

"She was unaware that Adeline had used it as collateral to procure a large loan from you. Did you ever tell any of this to Lan?"

"No. Absolutely not."

"So, if you didn't tell her, how come a few days later she was all calm about the subject? If she still didn't know where it was, she should have been in hysterics."

It only took a moment for Anthony to deduce, "Murray must have told her."

"Or," Suzanne reasoned. "Murray gave it to her."

"Why would he…" Anthony stopped himself, and he nodded his head. "Yeah, I guess I can see that."

"There were only two people that Murray truly cared about, Adeline and Lan. Did you know that Lan had introduced them?"

"Yes, Lan told me. Many times. She was very proud of the fact."

"Murray and Lan go far back. He cared for her very much. It's very conceivable that after buying the ring back from you, he gave it to Lan."

"I see," Anthony agreed.

"I hate admitting this, but I believe that Murray was intent on killing himself. If he kept the ring in his procession, it would have gone to his stepson. But what would have been the point in that? I think he bought it back from you, with the intention of giving it to Lan."

"Ahh... now I see." Anthony said and drank more coffee. "You're worried that if Lan has the ring, that she

may have sold it and squandered the proceeds gambling in Las Vegas."

Suzanne nodded.

"Addicts are all too capable of doing the unthinkable." Anthony drained his cup. "I'll be in Nevada in two days, and I hope you're wrong."

"Me too."

Chapter

22

Tuesday, December 15th, morning

"**I**'m afraid the poison was in the jam, again."

Charles was still in bed, when the telephone rang. Staff Sergeant Laval sounded as though he'd already drunk several cups of coffee, although Suzanne did note a hint of fatigue in his voice. He' s not getting enough sleep, she noted. It was the mother in her, she couldn't turn it off.

"I swear I gave you all the jam that I made this year," Suzanne said and rubbed her temples. She had not slept well either. Two nights in a row.

"I believe you," he said.

"Thank you. Do you know if Dariya and Walter will be alright?"

Laval paused before divulging, "Mr. Underhill is in stable condition. Unfortunately, due to Ms.

Underhill's pre-existing medical ailment, the kidney disease that you are already aware of, her situation is far more critical."

"Oh dear God," Suzanne said. "Who could have done this?"

"I, of course, am very interested in discovering the answer to that very question and I have interviewed many of your neighbours. I must warn you about something. If you were to be tried in the court of public opinion, they would have hung you by now."

"I don't care about what other people think."

"I know, but you need to, at least a little bit. A person's reputation is very important."

Suzanne understood that Laval wanted very much to be perceived as a righteous and bright police officer. Such vanity was reserved for the young. To her, the pursuit of the truth was far more critical than her social standings. It's probably why Regina made for a better politician than she did. She had learnt the hard way that people vote for the gleam of empty campaign promises over the stability of a proven track record.

But this wasn't politics. Solving Adeline's murder wasn't a job for a politician. She had lost several public battles to Regina in the past, but she would not be bested again. The truth was on her side, and public opinion was irrelevant.

She decided to ask the young staff sergeant a question that perhaps she shouldn't have, "Do you suspect me of poisoning the Underhills?"

"No," he said without hesitation.

"Why not, everyone else thinks that I could have done it?"

"Simple really, the tainted jam was a mix of blueberries and blackberries."

"I made blackberry jam this year." Suzanne reviewed something in her mind before saying, "Two summers ago it was very hot and dry. It was a bad year for the local blackberries. I couldn't pick enough of them, so I had to buy blueberries from the farmers' market. Two years ago was the only time I've ever made blackberry and blueberry jam."

"Ms. Rickson, I have some bad news for you," Laval said in a solemn tone. "Walter and Dariya Underhill weren't big fans of the jam."

"Very funny." Suzanne said dryly.

"The killer found last year's jam in the Underhill's fridge and poisoned it in hopes that it would once again implicate you."

"I see what you're saying," Suzanne considered it a viable theory. She thought about it and started to consider its ramifications. "It's possible that someone poisoned their jam months ago. Dariya and Walter weren't eating it, so they never got sick."

"It is conceivable, Ms. Rickson," Laval said, his voice full of enthusiasm. "At this point, I'd say there are a great number of possible scenarios. All we know for sure is the Underhills, for whatever reason, decided to have your jam on their toast yesterday morning. It could have been poisoned months ago or perhaps the night before last."

Suzanne nodded and remained silent.

"I would like to share with you a confidential piece of information, that I shouldn't be telling you," Laval continued. "The Underhills were not poisoned by a cardiac glycoside, as Ms. Wong was. The doctors believe that they ingested antifreeze."

"That's really interesting. Why would the killer change poisons?" Suzanne wondered out loud.

"I agree. It does seem to be a strange irregularity," Laval said. "I trust that you will keep this little secret to yourself. It could jeopardize our investigation if you don't."

"Of course," Suzanne said. "Staff Sergeant Laval, have I ever told you that I truly appreciate the fact that you are in charge of this case."

"Thank you, Ms. Rickson," Laval said. It was clear that he liked being acknowledged for being good as his job. "Have you considered that many of these scenarios raise the possibility of a major twist in our case?"

"How so?"

"It goes to motive. It's possible that the killer's primary objective wasn't to harm Ms. Wong and the Underhills. Perhaps the killer's goal is to frame you."

Laval has discovered what she had known from the start. This has always been a personal battle between Regina and herself. The end game is finally at hand, and it was time to tell Laval everything. She told him about her history and vendetta with Regina. He listened intently, never once interrupting her. She told him about the conversation which she'd overheard. He was particularly intrigued to learn that Regina had access to everyone's suite.

"That explains a lot," he said.

"So what do we do next?" Suzanne asked.

"Nothing," he answered. "It's a police matter now. You have been extremely helpful, Ms. Rickson. But from this point forward, there are certain procedures that I must adhere to, or the court case will get thrown out. You understand, don't you?"

"I do," she said.

That makes sense. Everything is in Laval's capable hands now. It's almost over.

"I do have to ask you one question if you don't mind," Laval said.

"Anything."

"It's a tad tawdry, I'm afraid," he warned.

"In that case, you definitely have to ask." Her curiosity piqued.

"It's about Byron Snow," Laval said. "There is a rumour that he had been having an affair, but your neighbours could only speculate with whom. Normally I would dismiss such hearsay, but I have learnt that if enough people believe in a rumour, there is often a grain of truth in it."

"You really shouldn't believe such things, Staff Sergeant. Have you been talking to Connie? She thinks that we're all stuck in an episode of Coronation Street and that everyone is secretly in bed with everyone else."

"I can only say it's a widespread rumour. Many people thought that the most likely person that Mr. Snow was seeing is his neighbour, Ms. Underhill."

"Pffft," Suzanne spat out. But then she remembered that all possibilities should be considered. "I wouldn't put it past Dariya. She and Walter have been in a loveless relationship for quite some time now. He's a drunk, and she's a nag. They're one of those couples that stayed together for the sake of their kids. And when their boys grew up and moved far away, Dariya wanted to leave Walter, but then they realized that they were close to being broke. They live together pretty much only for financial reasons. It's sad really."

Suzanne took a breath. She waited for Laval to say something, but he didn't, so she went on, "Byron, on the other hand, never. Don't ask me why, but he's smitten with Regina. She treats him like a little lap dog, and he obeys her every command. He'd be too scared to ever be unfaithful to her."

"Thank you, Ms. Rickson. You have been most helpful, and I very much value your insight."

"You're welcome Staff Sergeant," she said. "Can I ask you a favour now?"

"Please do."

"Yesterday you advised us not to go to the hospital, but would it be alright for me to go today? You see I'm awfully worried about Dariya. She doesn't deserve any of this." Suzanne's concerns were sincere, but she had an additional motive to speak to Dariya. She needed Dariya to confirm to Laval that Regina possessed a master key.

Laval took a moment before saying, "Why not. It should be perfectly fine today."

"Thank you so much, Staff Sergeant."

Suzanne made breakfast very loudly in hopes of waking Charles. She succeeded. He groaned as he trudged down the stairs. He was favouring his right side, it was clear that his left hip and knee were still sore. Charles appeared to be in a foul mood, but the smell of frying bacon quickly turned his spirits around.

"What's the occasion?" he asked.

"No occasion. It's a simple token to show my appreciation for you."

"Bacon served twice in a month. No, something's up." He stood behind her and eyed the three scrumptious strips that were just starting to coil in the frying pan.

"I think I have Regina right where I want her. And Laval is on board." Breakfast was ready. She wiped away the excess fat from the bacon and placed them beside a slice of toast and fresh-cut cantaloupe. "Sit, sit, everything is already done."

Charles sat down in his chair. A hot cup of green tea was already on the table for him. A smile grew on his face. "How did you get Laval to agree with you?" he asked.

"That's the beauty of it, I didn't. He got there on his own." After serving her husband, Suzanne prepared a bowl of hot oatmeal and sat down opposite him. All along she re-counted her telephone conversation with Laval.

"Ah, so mystery solved," Charles said when she was done.

"Not completely, but almost."

"Not your mystery, dear," he said. "My mystery. The Case of the Bacon Breakfast. Answer: you're in a good mood."

"Or perhaps I'm trying to knock you off by feeding you excessive amounts of sodium nitrite and saturated fats. Did you ever consider that?"

"It's not murder if the victim is happy to eat it. We can't live forever so we may as well live happily." Charles devoured his breakfast.

The Ricksons drove to the hospital just after eleven. They were surprised to discover that Dariya was no longer there. She had been airlifted to another hospital. The receptionist was unable to tell them anything else.

"Is her family aware of this?" Suzanne asked.

"Of course they are," the receptionist said.

Suzanne scowled. She ignored the receptionist's rudeness and asked, "Are we able to visit Mr. Underhill?"

Perhaps Walter could be of assistance. He could verify Dariya's story since he had been present too. She also had so many questions for him. The most important being, "Prior to yesterday, when was the last time you ate my jam?" His answer would help her complete the timeline of Regina's actions. It was crucial that Suzanne got all her ducks in a row.

Walter was in a private room on the second floor. Suzanne was in such a rush that they took the stairs because the elevator was taking too long.

As they approached Walter's room, Suzanne spotted an RCMP officer stationed outside his open door. It wasn't an officer she knew. She stood dead in her tracks. Something clicked in Suzanne. In a sudden flash of clarity, she realized that she had gotten plenty of things wrong. She had to re-evaluate everything. "How could I have been so blind?" she whispered out loud.

"You're not blind. What are you talking about?"

"Not that kind of blind, you oaf," Suzanne said. "Listen, I need to see Walter on my own first."

"Why?"

"Because I've been a fool and now I have to fix it." She explained a bit more, and Charles agreed to wait in the lobby.

"Good luck and be careful," he said as she walked away.

"Of course, dear."

"I can't let you in Ma'am," the guard said as she tried to pass him.

He was young and still showed signs of acne. He probably just graduated from the academy, Suzanne surmised. "Poppycock, I've spoken to Staff Sergeant Laval, and he authorized me to speak to Mr. Underhill." Technically that was true. Laval did say that she could visit.

"It's okay, Constable," Walter said from his bed. He was connected to a saline drip, but otherwise he looked to be in remarkably good health.

"I guess it's alright," the officer decided and stepped aside.

"Walter, how are you feeling," she said jovially as she entered.

"Much better, thank you. Please sit down." Walter motioned to a chair beside the bed. "Where's Chuck?"

She had already planned her little fib and responded, "Can you believe it, there was no parking outside. Poor Charles agreed to park at the grocery store and meet us here. Don't worry, he shouldn't take too long."

"Don't lie, Suzanne. You've always been poor at it," he said with a sly smile. "You two just didn't want to pay for parking. Chuck drove to the store's lot just to save a few bucks."

Suzanne didn't like being called cheap, but she kept her cool. "Walter, the parking here is free. It's not the big city."

"Oh," he said. "If you say so." The smirk disappeared from his face.

"How's Dariya?" Suzanne asked. "Nobody will tell me anything."

"She'll be alright, I hope. They flew her to Victoria this morning. There are complications with her kidneys, you see. And well, apparently there's this hotshot young doctor in their ICU. A Dr. Zaid. They say he's brilliant and that she'll be in good hands."

"She's in God' hands now," Suzanne said with a sigh. Having to be airlifted all the way to Victoria wasn't a good sign.

"Yeah, I guess she's in God's hands too."

"Walter, you used to be so religious, why did you stop coming to church on Sundays?"

"Do you know why God rested on Sunday?" Walter asked.

"I don't know. Why?" Suzanne didn't really still believe in creationism, but she felt the need to coax Walter and keep him at ease. She let him play his silly game.

"Same reason as me. The NFL was on."

"You do realize that the world is far older than football."

"It's a joke, Suzanne. Lighten up." Walter grinned and shifted his weight a bit.

"I'll try." She was not amused. But she kept her end game in mind.

"Listen," he said and toned his voice down to a more sombre level. "I have to apologize for yesterday, when I hollered out that you did this. I don't know what came over me. I wasn't in my right mind."

"Apology accepted," she said. "It was the ethylene glycol. It can have an intoxicating effect on people." Suzanne assumed that Laval's little revelation wasn't meant to be a secret from Walter. Surely, he had been informed as to what he had consumed. Also it didn't matter, the jig was already up.

Walter looked puzzled. "The what?"

"You had ingested antifreeze," she explained. "Many of its effects are similar to being drunk." She almost said, you should know that feeling, but she held her tongue. "If treated immediately, a patient should make a complete recovery. Luckily, you called 911 as soon as you were feeling ill."

"Yeah, that young sergeant was here this morning. He explained to me that antifreeze was mixed in with our jam. He said that Dariya would have recovered just like me, if it wasn't for her already weakened kidneys. It's possible that she'll have complete kidney failure. Oh, God no."

"She'll be alright, Walter," she reassured him. "Can I ask you a question?"

"Sure, of course."

"Who's Dariya's favourite author?"

Walter didn't have to think about that one. "Charlotte Bronte, of course. You know that she loves *Jane Eyre*."

"I do," Suzanne agreed. "She idolizes Bronte and quotes from her constantly."

"So why do you ask?"

"Because about a week ago Dariya, Regina and I had a conversation. We were talking about books. Dariya and I were trying to convince Regina that she should read more. Very oddly, Dariya recommended Nathaniel Hawthorne."

"So," Walter asked, puzzled.

"It seems like a minor detail, and at first it only bothered me a little bit, but none the less it still bothered me. Why would Dariya, who loved Bronte, advise someone to read Hawthorne?"

"It's really not that big a deal." Walter sounded annoyed.

"Ah, but it is," Suzanne said. "Do you know what Nathaniel Hawthorne's most celebrated work is?"

"No, and I don't care."

"You should," Suzanne said. It was her turn to smile. "It's *The Scarlet Letter.*"

"So."

Suzanne was a little disappointed with Walter's lack of knowledge regarding literature. "*The Scarlet Letter* is about a woman who has to wear a large 'A' patched onto her dress as a punishment for adultery."

Walter didn't say anything, so Suzanne continued to explain. "Dariya was being uncharacteristically subtle. She was accusing Regina of being an adulteress."

"You really think so?" Walter twitched, and his pupils dilated.

"I'm a tad ashamed to have taken so long to figure it out. I have to admit my vision has been clouded. But I see better now. Everything is starting to fit into place." She paused for effect. "So Walter, I have to ask, how long have you been sleeping with Regina?"

"What?" Walter cried out. "Why would you think I was with Regina?"

"Forgive me. I already know the answer. You started your affair approximately eighteen months ago. That's when you stopped going to church," she responded. "Every Sunday morning, Byron goes bird watching; rain or shine. He's gone for hours. And as long as Dariya went with us to mass, it was a perfect time for you to rendezvous with Regina."

Walter tried to get out of bed, but he was hindered by the saline drip. "I don't care what you think. It's all circumstantial," he protested.

"Yeah, you're right," she said. "What I think is rather irrelevant. But the opinion of Staff Sergeant Laval is far more important. It's him who placed an officer outside of your door. The guard's not here to protect you, but rather to ensure you don't get away. You'll be arrested soon enough." Suzanne got up to leave. She didn't want to be around Walter any longer than she had to be. She was embarrassed to have been so narrow-sighted. She had been so sure that Regina had poisoned Dariya to silence her that she had forgotten that husbands were the most likely suspect for crimes against women. Walter wasn't the first husband to poison himself in order to alleviate suspicion.

"Wait," he pleaded from his bed. "You're right about Regina and me. And yes, I poisoned Dariya. She found out about my affair and was going to divorce me. I was alright with that. But when Regina decided to leave me too. It was too much. I cracked."

"You don't have to explain yourself to me. I'm not on the jury."

"But I didn't touch Adeline. You have to believe me."

"I do," Suzanne said her back turned to him as she left.

"Oh, don't sound so righteous. I know that you want to nail Regina for Adeline's death. But it couldn't have been her. She was with me on the morning that Adeline was poisoned. It's just like you said, we were together every Sunday."

"I believe you," Suzanne said and walked out to meet Charles. She looked towards the young officers poised outside the door, wanting to ensure that he'd heard Walter's confession. The officer nodded.

Chapter

23

Mid-afternoon

Sitting in the Halfmoon Bay Cafe, Suzanne sipped on a strong coffee. The tiny café was renowned for its homemade soup and cozy décor. It was a popular meeting spot for the locals and made for an excellent neutral zone.

After leaving the hospital, the Ricksons had returned to their home. Suzanne immediately phoned Regina, and the two of them had agreed to meet at the café for 2:30. Suzanne had arrived early and got herself a beverage. She sat patiently and tried to relax.

Regina was already fifteen minutes late, but Suzanne wasn't surprised. Regina was like a rattlesnake, fighting for any tiny advantage that she can grasp. Showing up late was Regina's tactic of trying to control the meeting, but it can only work if Suzanne allowed herself to be annoyed by it. She knew to expect dozens of similar strategies from Regina. It doesn't matter. Suzanne was confident that none of them would be effective. The mere fact that Regina had agreed to meet was proof that she was desperate and that the war had already been won.

This meeting is unnecessary, Suzanne told herself. Perhaps it was vain of her to have requested it. She mustn't gloat. But in the end, it was fitting that they should have their final showdown.

Suzanne had chosen the table wisely. It was at the back of the restaurant, near a large stand-up freezer that held individually packaged frozen soups to go. The buzz of the freezer was barely audible over the soothing jazz music that played in the background. From where she sat, Suzanne could see the entire restaurant. It was as secluded as the tiny café could offer.

When Regina finally walked through the doorway, she scanned the coffeehouse. At best the Halfmoon Bay Cafe could seat twenty patrons, but at this time of day, it was almost empty. She nodded hello to a gentleman in a plaid overcoat. The man returned the nod but quickly turned his back to her. She pivoted to greet Suzanne and the two adversaries locked eyes.

Suzanne did not expect an apology for her tardiness, and she did not get one. Instead Regina opened with simple rudeness. "Oh, there you are, Suzy. I almost didn't see you."

Suzanne knew better than to react to Regina's discourtesy. "Thank you for agreeing to meet me."

With that, Regina spun around and ignored Suzanne as she engaged in conversation with the barista, Lucy, and ordered and a coffee. Suzanne sat in silence.

After several minutes, Regina turned back around and addressed Suzanne. "I have to admit that I'm very curious as to what is so urgent that you insisted we talk immediately."

"I thought we needed to clear the air between us," Suzanne explained.

"Great, I half expected to come here and find a nondescript police officer sitting just close enough to overhear our conversation."

"No, Regina, no tricks like that. It's just a friendly meeting. I felt that it was time that we both put our cards on the table and see this through." Suzanne caught Lucy eyeing them from behind her counter. Suzanne sensed that she was being spied upon even though Lucy was doing her best not to appear as so. Surely, Lucy was aware of their long-time feud and would be curious as to why they were meeting in her establishment. She must have felt like a saloon owner in the Wild West when two rival cowboys sat down at the same card table.

"You're not going to start accusing me of killing Adeline again, are you? We've been through this. I have an alibi and no motive to harm her." Regina raised her voice to ensure all those present could hear her.

"No, I know you're not the murderer," Suzanne said calmly. "You can relax. There's no reason to cause a scene."

Regina straightened her blouse and said but a single word, "Good."

"I know that you had an alibi on the Sunday in which Adeline was poisoned. I just came from the hospital and had a fascinating talk with him."

Regina's eyes widened. "What? Byron's not in the hospital. What are you going on about?"

"Stop playing games, Regina. It's far too late for that. When Byron claimed that you were home all Sunday, tending to him while he was sick, I was convinced that it was because he wanted to provide you with an alibi. But I've just learnt that you had one all along; you just couldn't admit to it. In actuality, it was your husband who needed to fabricate an account of his whereabouts." Suzanne had been formulating this speech for hours. She realized that she was getting a little too wordy and she was starting to sound a smidge over-dramatic, like Nero Wolfe or Perry Mason. She was enjoying herself.

"What are you saying? Byron would never hurt anyone." Regina's face twisted ever so slightly. Suzanne knew that she had struck a nerve. Good, it's working.

"That's what everyone would think. He's not the type of guy that one would place high on any suspect list. But a desperate, heart-broken man is capable of a great many things."

"No, Byron would never hurt anyone," Regina repeated.

"Oh, don't act shocked Regina. I'm fairly certain that you've known for quite some time. Byron designed it for you to figure out and you did. You've been protecting him ever since. The sad thing is that it was all because of you. Everything that has happened to Adeline and Dariya was for you."

Regina slammed her coffee cup down. "I didn't cause any this. You have nothing on me."

"That's true. I can't prove anything, but please hear me out."

Suzanne watched Regina's eyes shift, and her lips fidget. Her nemesis was clearly playing everything out in her head, trying to imagine how much Suzanne had uncovered. Regina finally said, "Alright then, I'll listen."

Suzanne licked her lips before saying, "Byron discovered that you were having an affair with Walter. Don't deny it, because Walter has already admitted everything to me."

There was no response from Regina. She surely knew that the jig was up, but she was still trying to calculate a way in which she could walk away unscathed. It was her nature.

"Your husband poisoned Adeline because he thought that she was a threat to you. It was all a cruel, yet grand gesture, to regain your love and respect," Suzanne said.

"Byron always had my love and respect."

"Sadly, that's not true. For if it had been, Adeline would still be alive." Suzanne stared deep into her rivals' eyes, and Regina turned quickly away. "Remember when you came to me with the flowers after Adeline's death. You revealed that you had collected a bunch of proxy letters. I wasn't that surprised that you had rigged the elections, it's the kind of thing I expected from you. I may not have been overly shocked, but Byron definitely was. I realize now that it was the first time in which he had heard of your scheming. If you had filled him in earlier, he would have known that Adeline wasn't going to win the election and that there was no point of him taking her out of the way for you."

Regina's face turned a little paler. "If you expect me to turn on Byron, you're completely mistaken! You don't have any proof."

"I don't need proof. I'm not the law. This is just between you and me. And in such, I want you to think of something else."

"Nothing you can say will ever make me betray my Byron."

"We'll see, Regina." Suzanne was getting smug. She didn't want to appear as if she was gloating, but inside she definitely was. She had waited a great many years for this moment to come. She had well prepared to deliver a knockout blow. "It's the poison he used, lily of the valley. You see, it grows everywhere, and it's not hard to procure. That is, in the summer it's not hard to get. But the plant dies in the autumn, lies dormant in the winter and re-grows in the spring."

"Get to your point. I'm not here for a horticultural lesson."

Suzanne didn't let the interruption disturb her. She continued, "Byron had to have collected the poison months ago, before the election campaign even started, before he could have deemed Adeline as your political rival. He had to have picked the petals and harvested the poison in the fall and Adeline couldn't have been his initial target."

Suzanne drained her coffee because she wanted to give Regina time to think things through for herself. After the pause Suzanne continued. "No, his intention was a lot more passionate. He had originally planned on killing you. You see, he was dejected. Maybe he planned on killing Walter too, but that would have been harder for the louse rarely left his home. Or maybe he planned on feeding it to you and himself at the same time. A murder-suicide. Maybe he wanted to die too. You'll have to ask him that yourself. But either way, he couldn't go through with it. So he kept the poison and schemed up a new plan."

Regina said nothing, so Suzanne continued. "Surely you'd appreciated the fact that he killed off your main political rival. But Byron also knew that if he did, a great deal of suspicion would fall upon you. So he organized two things in advance. He created an alibi for both of you, by feigning sickness and making everyone believe that he was bedridden during the time of the crime. On the day of the murder, he told you that he was well enough to go bird watching like he always did on Sundays. And just like you did every Sunday, while he was out and Dariya was at mass, you snuck over to Walter's. At this time Byron used the master key that you kept, to access Adeline's home and poisoned the jam. Only after Adeline was found near dead at home, did he start telling everyone of his and your alibi. I assume that it was about then that you pieced it all together. At that point you would have had two choices: to collaborate his lie or to turn him in."

The two women were watching each other intensely. Suzanne had anticipated Regina to be denying everything, but she wasn't. Lucy appeared and broke the silence by asking,

"Either of you want a refill?"

"No, we're fine," Regina blurted out.

"Actually, I'd love a refill, if you don't mind. You make the best coffee, Lucy."

"Oh, thank you, hon."

Lucy filled Suzanne's cup with her typical breezy manner. "You sure you don't want more Reggie? It's a fresh brew."

"Yes, I'm sure. Thank you though."

"I'm right here if you change your mind."

They waited for Lucy to step back behind her counter.

Suzanne started up again, "So now you're committed. And Byron reveals to you his second plan, one that he had already set in motion weeks before. He knows that you'll love it. Byron tells you how he had attempted to frame me. He had used the same key to access my home weeks in advance and stole my library card. With it, he borrowed the book regarding the poisons. The next phase was to sneak back into my home, plant the book and inform the police."

Regina shook her head as if trying to deny everything, but unable to do so with words. Suzanne pressed on. "I'm sure you agreed. Along with the motive, which you had created years ago: Charles's fictitious liaison with Adeline and the fact that it was my jam that had been tainted; it should have been enough to frame me as the murderer. I have to admit, a lesser detective may have come to that conclusion, but I was very fortunate that the newly arrived Staff Sergeant Laval headed this case, and he did not fall for Byron's ruse."

"You can't prove any of this," Regina spewed, anger seething from her every word.

"So you keep repeating. But as I said on numerous occasions, it's not I who is tasked with proving anything. It's Staff Sergeant Laval's job to substantiate your involvement in these crimes, and I feel he's been a step ahead of even myself all along. He, no doubt, has come to the same conclusion as I have, and he has far more resources at his disposal to prove his case.

"And there is one instant which substantiates to your involvement in this plot. It's when Byron almost ran over Charles. I realize now that only you could have orchestrated such a political move. Sure it was meant at as a warning, but why not also make it an opportunity it discredit me. You had heard of my suspicions about your son's vehicle being present on that Sunday. So Byron rented a vehicle that matched the description and nearly ran Charles over with it. I assume that he didn't intend on hurting Charles. You had calculated that I'd lash out and accuse you and your son, and you'd quickly disprove my allegation. It was social engineering for the sole purpose of humiliating me."

"Don't you feel so self-righteous," Regina spat out.

"I'm not. In fact, I'm embarrassed. I should have solved all of this earlier, if I had, perhaps I could have saved Dariya. You see, I was so convinced early on that you were behind everything that my vision was clouded. If I saw logically from the beginning, I might have figured it out before Walter, being the weasel that he is, poisoned Dariya.

"Sadly, that too was all for you. By returning your affections to Byron, your new lover, Walter, felt betrayed. He must have seen through Byron's lie and knew that he was guilty. I'm not sure why Walter didn't turn your husband in at the time, but I assume it was because he didn't want to implicate you. So instead, he took the opportunity to get rid of his wife and try and win you back. He figured that if he accomplished an equally grand gesture as Byron's, perhaps it would be enough to sway you back to him. I don't know what kind of spell you had cast of these two men, but they were both willing to murder innocent women, in order to gain your affection. It's really twisted."

With that said, Suzanne got up to leave. She wanted to put everything behind her. It was all over. Surely Staff Sergeant Laval had already arrested Byron.

Regina sat silently. Clearly, there was no fight left in her. She probably had never really taken a moment to consider herself the catalyst for all that had occurred. She had been too busy protecting Byron. The threats, the smokescreens and the red herrings were most likely all her doing. Was she careful enough never to have incriminated herself? Deep down inside Suzanne knew that her devoted husband would fall on his sword for her and she'd scheme her way out of prosecution. I may have won this battle, Suzanne surmised, but our feud is far from over.

Chapter

24

Saturday, January the 3rd, night

Suzanne and Charles returned to a cold home as the thermostat had been turned off for the past two weeks. They had asked Connie to occasionally come in and water the plants, and it appeared as though she had. Their reliable friends would have looked after Nero too, but they had too many pet birds to have a dog in their house. Poor Nero had to spend the holidays in the kennel. He's going to be very upset with them when they pick him up tomorrow.

While Charles was igniting the pilot light on their furnace, Suzanne put on the kettle. They were both exhausted and thrilled to be back in their quiet home. They loved spending the Christmas break with all their family. Suzanne had been just as surprised as everyone else when Mark appeared at Christmas Eve. The boys were ecstatic to see their father and Lisa almost cried. Four generations of Suzanne's family were re-united and spent the holidays together under one giant roof. Her father had long ago refused to sell the family stead. He insisted on keeping it even though it was far too big for him and worth a tiny fortune. Despite his family's pleas, he had re-mortgaged the house and spent the money to retain regular maintenance. He swore that the only way he'd leave his home was on a stretcher. Tenacity ran in the family, and it stemmed from its patriarch, who was perhaps the most stubborn of them all.

Suzanne had very much enjoyed spending time in her childhood home. It was two weeks that she would cherish forever. But at the same time, she had forgotten just how loud a household with youngsters can be. Her grandchildren had so much energy. They were like bees. Lisa had kept reminding Suzanne that her boys were very well behaved and received excellent grades in school. Still, Suzanne thought that they ran out of control and had very little respect for the older generations. She had stopped counting the times Lisa said, "That's just how kids are nowadays."

Tea was set, and the Rickson's sat down to review their mail. Connie and Ivan had been collecting their letters and stacking them by the front door. "Wow it really piles up in a couple of weeks," Charles remarked.

"It's probably mostly junk mail."

"It can wait for tomorrow."

"Agreed," Suzanne said with a yawn.

✳✳✳✳

Suzanne slept until eight the next morning. Charles was fidgety. "Are you up?" she asked.

"I can't sleep anymore. I guess it's the jetlag,"

An hour later and Charles was washing the breakfast dishes while Suzanne dried. She spotted Connie and Ivan stroll by. "No doubt they were looking for signs of life; checking to see if we're were up yet."

Charles waved to them through the window and beckoned them to come in.

"We didn't want to phone and possibly wake you up," Connie said at the doorway.

"You two are absurdly sweet," Charles said, holding the front door open wide.

"Would you like some tea?" Suzanne offered.

It wasn't until everyone was settled at the table that Suzanne asked, "Did you hear from Anthony? Do you know if he found Lan in Las Vegas?"

"No, we haven't received word from him or even from Lanny for that matter," said Ivan.

"I'm surprised you haven't asked us anything about Regina yet." Connie grinned.

"I was stalling the unpleasantness and hoping for good news first."

"We're sorry about Lan. She's a lost soul, and I fear that we'll never hear from her again," Ivan said while looking down at his mug.

Connie sighed and rubbed her knuckle. "Well, perhaps the Ice Queen is also out of our lives. She hasn't been seen or heard of since Lord Byron was arrested."

"They would be holding Byron in a detention centre in Vancouver," Suzanne said. "Regina is probably staying at her son's home for now. She'll be back once Byron has been tried and thrown in a permanent prison, which could be anywhere in the province. Perhaps she'll move out in order to remain close to her husband."

"Oh, hopefully you're right," Connie said. "Do you think that they'll charge Regina with conspiracy after the fact?"

"If they haven't done it yet, I doubt they will," Suzanne said. She had forced herself not to think about Regina while on vacation with her family. But she had asked Caroline to keep an eye on it for her. She was upset when her daughter never had anything to report. "Byron was very calculating and made sure that Regina couldn't be found guilty of anything."

"What about the attempt to run over Charles? Didn't you think she was guilty of that?" Ivan asked.

"The police have discovered that Byron had borrowed the pick-up truck from a friend for a few days," added Connie.

"Ah, so that's why he didn't hit Charles," Suzanne said. "He didn't want to damage the vehicle because it would have raised suspicions."

"That's the only reason he didn't hit me," Charles said. His face looked a little pale.

"I'm afraid so, dear." Suzanne patted her husband's back. "I'm sure the police won't discover any link between Regina and the borrowed vehicle. They won't be able to prove that she was involved in any way."

"That's a pity," Connie said. "Did you hear that Walter's been charged too, maybe he'll share a cell with Byron."

While in Montreal, Suzanne had been thrilled to receive a call from Dariya. She was still at the Victoria General Hospital, but she was stable and expected to make a full recovery. She wasn't even that shocked to learn that Walter had tried to kill her and that he was so easily caught. "Misery generates hate," Dariya had resorted to quoting Bronte again.

"I know you just got back, but are you going to Church today?" Connie asked.

"Of course we are," Suzanne said.

"We better let you go," Ivan smiled. "Give you time to get ready."

After their friends left, Suzanne and Charles sat back down at the table. Mass was in two hours, plenty of time to get ready. Suzanne was content with being caught up with the current affairs of her community. Justice would be served, and a sense of balance had been restored. Although she was still in shock from the death of her dear friend, at least she knew that the guilty party would be punished. First-degree murder in Canada had a sentence of life imprisonment.

As Charles was clearing the table, Suzanne decided to tackle the daunting pile of mail. She discarded the adverts, which consisted mostly of the last minute Christmas ideas and the thick flyers for boxing week blowouts. A separate stack was created for bills and one for Christmas cards that had arrived while they were away. One letter caught her attention; it was mailed from the US but had no return address. She opened it first.

To my dearest friend Suzanne,

Please don't hate me for needing to disappear. I lost my mind, and I couldn't go on as is. It's only now that I feel guilty for not tell you that I was leaving. I need to be free, to start over. But at the same time, I don't want you to worry about me. Please forget me.

My life is sad and insignificant. I do not matter. I can't do anything right. While riding the ferry to Vancouver, I decided to hurl a suitcase of Jei Jei's favourite clothes into the water. It was supposed to be my way of saying goodbye to her. But instead it turned into a major incident. Some other passengers heard the splash and assumed the worst. They stopped the ferry and conducted an investigation. I didn't want to admit to anything, because I thought I might get in trouble. Every time I try to do something good, it goes bad.

I have been so cruel and self-absorbed. So many people have reached out and tried to help me, but I have always been lost. My soul has been dead since that tragic night when the good Lord chose to take my husband and beautiful daughter away from me. I have never recovered and most likely never will.

And although my life may be inconsequential, the story of Murray Wilthe is worth telling. He was always a cherished friend. Murray has been eternally tied to me from the moment my Henry's car crashed into his truck.

At first, I blamed Murray for killing my family, but the police and the insurance company confirmed that Murray was 100%

faultless of the accident and that my husband had been intoxicated. What kind of man drives his daughter home from ballet class while being completely spaced-out on marijuana? The only man I ever loved. I sure know how to pick them.

You know already how Murray settled with ICBC and travelled abroad for many years. He returned a wealthy widower and a drunk. It must have been kismet that brought us together in group therapy. I knew who he was instantly. Feelings of regret, blame and sorrow filled my every thought. The sight of this man reminded me too much of my departed family, and the pain my husband had caused. It was Murray who befriended me. It was he who taught me that what was done was done. Or at least he tried to teach me that, but I could never truly learn it.

I've told you before how I had introduced Murray to Adeline. I wouldn't have called it love at first sight, or at least it wasn't for Adeline. Murray was a little different but he always had a heart of gold. And when he set his sights upon her, he used every ounce of goodness that he could muster to woo her. He was an incredibly kind, selfless and generous man. Over time Jei Jei saw this and in her own rights fell madly in love with him. Sadly, of her many traits, pig-headedness was her primary characteristic. She had long ago vowed to never marry again. Despite this Murray proposed. Adeline was overwhelmed and couldn't resist saying "yes". I was the first person she told about the proposal, and it was one of the happiest days of my life.

You also know that a few days later she told Murray that she couldn't marry him. She tried to give back the ring, and he refused. He said that it would always be hers. I was almost as devastated as he was. She had broken his heart, and it was entirely my fault. I thought that the love of a good man would have been enough for Adeline to annul her foolish vow of never marrying again. It wasn't as if Murray was poor. She wouldn't have needed Tony's alimony cheques anymore. Everyone could have been happy.

The whole affair sent Murray into a tailspin. He started drinking again. He moved out into the cabin in the woods, and he virtually disappeared for a few years. He was at a point in his life where I couldn't help him. No one could.

Jei Jei, on the other hand, took everything in stride. She didn't seem torn up by the changing of her decision. In fact, it seemed to give her life again. I can't explain it. She will always be my big sister, but I will never understand her.

I took to gambling again, and it was Jei Jei that pulled me out. She dragged me to

Gamblers Anon and kismet intervened for a second time in my life, for that is where I met, her ex-husband, the man who ruined her and would one day save me, Anthony. I don't know if she knew that he was a long-time member, or if she had arranged it for him to be my sponsor. She denied it when I asked her.

It took years, but for the first time in a long time, I felt as if I could breathe. Like a weight had been lifted from my chest, that I wasn't alone in this world. I was clean again.

Adeline helped me through Career College, where I learnt to be a dental hygienist. She got me my first job after school by talking to her dentist. When Jei Jei moved from the original units to the new Rosewood building of Secret Cove, Jei Jei suggested that I could buy her old flat. I told her that I had no money. She helped me secure a mortgage from the bank and loaned me the funds for the down payment.

What you probably don't know is something that I had only recently discovered myself. Adeline was nowhere near as wealthy as we all had assumed. She didn't have enough money to pay for my down payment. She approached Anthony and borrowed the money from him. She used Murray's engagement ring as a down payment, and she had been repaying him monthly by accepting a smaller monthly alimony cheque.

It wasn't until Murray came to see me after Jei Jei's death, that he explained her sacrifice for me. He had the ring with him, and he explained to me how he had repurchased it from Anthony. He wanted me to take it. I didn't understand until he said, "It's Adeline's ring, it will always be hers." He wanted me to bury it with her.

He said little else. Murray bowed to me, and I bowed back. That was the last time I ever saw him.

I didn't know what to do. I really needed the money. And selling the ring would have solved many of my problems. Five days later, I was still sitting on my couch, wondering what to do. That ring staring back at me from an overhanging shelf. Adeline would have wanted me to keep it, not lose it forever.

And then Anthony phoned. Everything changed. Murray was dead, and according to you, I was the last person to have seen him alive. He gave me the ring and then jumped into the ocean. He had trusted me to complete his last request, and I couldn't bear to do it.

One more thing that you might not know is that Robert and I go way back. Even though Murray had been estranged from his son for the past twelve years, I spoke to him regularly. I had been keeping Rob up to date with his father's wellbeing, or in many cases, his father's lack of wellbeing. After Murray's death, I had made arrangements with Robert to have his step father's ashes buried with Adeline. They're together now. Like they always should have been. Adeline has her ring, and Murray has her.

I'm living in Arizona for now. Robert kindly took me in after a brief relapse in Las Vegas. Don't worry about me. Murray is taking care of me, even after he's gone. I'll be alright.

Yours sincerely,

Lan

Suzanne folded the letter and handed it to Charles.

She got up and walked upstairs to get dressed. A tear rolled down her cheek. "I'm sorry that I ever doubted you, my worthy friend."

Acknowledgements

I'd like to thank my entire family for their support. They have always encouraged my desire to be a writer, and I wouldn't have been given this opportunity if it were not for them.

Growing up, my mother often encouraged me to read more, but I wasn't a fan. I remained ignorant of the beauty of literature until my grandmother gave me a copy of *Not A Penny More, Not a Penny Less*. Jeffery Archer was her favourite author, and she thought I might like him too. I read it within a week during a family camping trip, and I've been an avid reader ever since.

In college, my girlfriend changed my life when she told me that I should read Dostoevsky. Our relationship didn't last long, but my love for Russian Literature will remain with me forever. Thank you, Kamilla.

I wrote this book because my mother read my first novel, *Straight Men in Gay Bars*, and was horrified. I decided that my next work would be for her. To quote Monte Python, "And now for something completely different."

Suzanne and Charles Rickson aren't complete composites of my parents, but they are close. I did envision them when writing my protagonists.

The way they bicker and yet always have each other's back. My parents are quickly approaching their fiftieth anniversary and are still going strong (most of the time).

My beta readers often said they loved Charles. That's my dad, permanently jovial, constantly helping others and always there for you. My mom is the brains, approaching every problem in a pragmatic and logical manner. Together they make an exceptional team.

My friends and family often say that they were not surprised that I became a stay at home dad. Perhaps it was my destiny. A writer by day, a father/husband at night. Sure it's two full-time jobs, but I manage (most of the time). I often wake up at 5 am on weekends, just to get some writing done before everyone else wakes up. It can be a little much, but I wouldn't trade my life with anyone. Thank you to my beautiful wife, Stacia and two wonderful boys, Mason and Nikolas.

It's been said that friends are the family which we get to choose. Most of my friends are my peers within the Port Moody Writers Group. I have been bringing this story to them for years, and with their help, it was dissected and re-configured several times. I'd especially like to thank the instructors: Joyce Gram, who edited this novel, Debra Purdy Kong, whose books I love, and whose writing style I often try to mimic. Along with Eileen Kernaghan, Heather Conn, Deb Vail, and Julie Ferguson, all of whom have guided me on my way to being an author.

Dr. Omar Z. Ahmad proof-read my medical terms and hospital procedures. It's been a while since we spoke, so I hope I still got it all right.

A big thanks to all my murder buddies. I'm lucky to have so many sweet friends with twisted imaginations. It's a good thing we all chose to write about crime and not actually do the deeds. Thank you to Debra Purdy Kong (once again), AJ Devlin, Carlos Lozano and Lyn Ayre for all the fine-tuning.

To all my moms, all three of them, Madeleine, Marge and Shirley, thank you.

To my wife, to my friends and to my family, writing may be a solitary profession, but I couldn't do it without you.

Erik D'Souza is an author, publisher and promoter of the BC literary community.

To learn more about his writings, please visit erikdsouza.com.

To see more titles by Timbercrest Publishing, please go to timbercrestpublishing.com

Death in Halfmoon Bay is the first in a series of cozy/traditional mysteries chronicling the stories of Suzanne Rickson.

Her daughter, Caroline Rickson, will also face many challenges. But her stories are considerably darker. Look for *The Stanley Park Rapist* available soon by Timbercrest Publishing.

Made in the USA
Middletown, DE
03 July 2020